Consuming Fire

Catherine Fearns

CROOKED
CAT

Copyright © 2019 by Catherine Fearns
Artwork: goonwrite.com
Design: soqoqo
Editor: Jeff Gardiner
All rights reserved.

No part of this book may be used or reproduced in any manner
whatsoever without written permission of the author or Crooked
Cat Books except for brief quotations used for promotion or in
reviews. This is a work of fiction. Names, characters, and incidents
are used fictitiously.

First Black Line Edition, Crooked Cat, 2019

Discover us online:
www.crookedcatbooks.com

Join us on facebook:
www.facebook.com/crookedcat

Tweet a photo of yourself holding
this book to **@crookedcatbooks**
and something nice will happen.

Gift Aid item

BID:12041897

Praise for Catherine Fearns'
Reprobation

"Every so often, a book comes along that blows you away with its uniqueness. For me, Reprobation by Catherine Fearns is one of those books."

Readers' Favorite

"Reprobation by Catherine Fearns is the perfect example of plot twists and book club debate. Riveting, fast paced, even amusing, this novel is bound for the best seller list! Catherine Fearns could easily corner the market in the suspense genre."

Readers' Favorite

"While at heart a mystery thriller Reprobation is so much more than this. It's a novel about life, death, religion, the choices we make and the irreversible destinies we face. As it hurtles along to its spine-tingling conclusion you will not be able to put the book down. A truly remarkable and incredibly well-researched read."

Amazon customer

"Reprobation lures you in from the first pages. Featuring a nun and a death metal singer in the first pages, it was never going to be a run of the mill tale. The plot is well-crafted and the detail on Calvinism, metal and the study of death all well researched and integrated into the story. Despite the creepy cover, you need have little interest in theology or death metal to enjoy this novel immensely."

Simon Bower, author of *Dead In The Water*

"This book pulled me in right from the beginning. It seems like an odd mash-up: a nun, heavy metal band leader, and genetics, but it is perfectly balanced and gave me everything I never knew I needed in a novel."

Goodreads

"A thrilling crime novel that allows scope to think and be entertained with a mystery that is as dark as it is exciting. As complex as the DNA it alludes to at times. Totally engaging. Stunningly original and faultless in its plotting. The best news is a second book is scheduled to be released as early as February 2019. I for one cannot wait, and on the strength of this debut I expect the name of Catherine Fearns on every crime fiction fan's lips, the next go to author and a fresh talent we all want to read!"

Amazon customer

"Not only did the book surprise me in the quality of its writing, the depth of the characters and beautifully descriptive landscapes Fearns paints of her native Liverpool, but I found the explorations of philosophy and religion to lend it a depth that such novels very scarcely display. It was such a compelling read, that for the first time in a while I read it cover to cover in one sitting. For a first time novelist, this is seriously impressive work, I highly recommend it!"

Amazon customer

"I love a book that pulls me right in like this and entertains, yet at the same time opens my mind to ideas I'd never thought about before. With an unusual cast of characters, wonderful writing and a layered plot, this is a story that will stay with me for a very long time."

Heidi Catherine, author of The Soulweaver series"

"Quite a revelation… fascinating to read.. an immensely brave novel"

Amazon customer

For John

About the Author

Catherine Fearns is from Liverpool, UK. Her first novel, Reprobation, was published by Crooked Cat Books in October 2018. As a music journalist she has written for *Pure Grain Audio, Broken Amp* and *Noisey*. Her short fiction and non-fiction has appeared in *Offshoots, Toasted Cheese, Succubus, Here Comes Everyone* and *Metal Music Studies*. She has a degree in History from Oxford University and a Masters from the London School of Economics, and prior to becoming a writer she worked as a financial analyst and breastfeeding counsellor. She lives in Geneva with her husband and four children.

Acknowledgements

Thank you Laurence and Steph Patterson at Crooked Cat Books, for your continued support and belief in my writing. Thank you to my editor Jeff Gardiner; so happy to work with you again.

Thank you to my beta readers for your honest and insightful comments on early drafts of this book: John Campos, David Meldrum, Dorothy Roussen, Paul Tod and Louise Braddock. Thank you Rebecca Bradley for your police procedural advice; Laura and Matthew Gowen for advice on legal matters.

It's been a wild ride since the publication of Reprobation, and I'd like to thank everyone who took the time to read and review my debut novel. I feel very lucky to belong to such a wonderful, diverse community of writers, readers, musicians and friends. It's been a pleasure to interact with so many new people this year, both in person and virtually.

I'd like to say a special thank you to the following who have gone out of their way to support me: Bob Stone at Write Blend, Sam Missingham at Lounge Books, Clare Mackintosh, Ben Cameron, Rachel Gilbey at Rachel's Random Resources, Adrian Magson at Writing Magazine, all at UK Crime Book Club and Radio Merseyside.

Consuming Fire

'...ye shall all perish by a terrifying and horrible death... a fire shall devour you on every side and utterly crush you, and by the power of God a flame shall go forth from His Mouth which shall burn ye up and reduce ye unto nothing in Hell.'

The Key Of Solomon The King, Book 1 Chapter VII

'The Avvites made Nibhaz and Tartak, and the Sepharvites burned their children in the fire as sacrifices to Adrammelech and Anammelech, the gods of Sepharvaim.'

2 Kings 17:31

'First appeared Adramelech, a spirit in guile and malice exceeding Satan, against whom his bosom still boiled with indignant rage, for being the first who attempted the apostasy, which he himself had long before projected. The actions he performed were not to advance Satan's kingdom, but his own. From years immemorial he had been considering how to raise himself to the dominion of hell; how to engage the prince of the fiery deep in a fresh war against the Eternal: how to cause him to be forever banished to the infinite space: or, if all failed, how he might subdue him by force of arms.'

Friedrich Gottlieb Klopstock, The Messiah, Book II, 1808

Preface to the 1879 translation of the Ars Adramelechum

It is with far more trepidation than pride that I present, to whomsoever it may concern, this modern English translation of the Ars Adramelechum. In full awareness that I denigrate the words of this strange, majestic and terrifying text by adding my own inferior contribution, I am convinced it would be remiss of me not to prepare the reader for what is to follow. And, moreover, to entreat the reader to resist going beyond this introduction. Be faint of heart; do not succumb to the bombast that afflicted me and which can only end in hubris. For while it was my mortal duty to commit this work to posterity, my task has also been my destruction. Further mortal warnings are to be found below, but it is perhaps easiest, in the beginning, if I provide the reader with a faithful delineation of how this mysterious tome came into my hands.

In 1875 I took up a position as lecturer in the History Department at the University of Geneva, my first appointment after graduating in theology from Oxford. My remit was to conduct research on how the communities of the Jura region, on the border between France and Switzerland, had maintained their Catholic traditions in the face of post-Reformation persecution. As Protestant severity swept across parts of Europe in the sixteenth and seventeenth centuries, enclaves of devotees clung to the magic of the Catholic faith. Their practices were conducted in secret, shrouded in mysticism, hostile to outsiders, and consequently little had been done before now to document this particular consequence of the Reformation. For months I endeavoured in my task, visiting churches and burying myself in libraries, but I confess that my initial alacrity was soon oppressed by a debilitating ennui. Whilst my subject was not in itself tedious, quite the contrary, I was consumed by loneliness in this foreign country where I struggled with the French language. Worse still, I was becoming increasingly aware that I myself was a tedious subject, as it were. I was utterly unloved by my students, a rowdy rabble far more interested in frequenting the opium dens and brothel houses of the Old Town of Geneva than attending my tutorials. One evening I found myself drowning my sorrows at the bar of La Clémence when I overheard a group of young people in uproarious laughter over the tiresome dreariness of their tutor Le Pré Anglais. I must own that I spent some minutes trying to convince myself otherwise, but this insufferable Pré they were mocking was none other than myself. I daresay it was at this moment I took the decision to make something of my researches that these frivolous young people could not possibly accuse of dreariness.

On the fringes of my study had always been the knowledge that the Jura border communities had managed to maintain their Catholicism by blending it with ancient Celtic traditions. In a region famed for witchcraft, this paganism would seem to border on the occult, and so until now I had felt it anathema to my theological work. But I now wondered if I could perhaps use it to entice my students; even the word itself - 'occult' - is so deliciously forbidden. Through whispers and gossip in the churches I visited, I heard of one village in particular, an isolated hamlet not far from Geneva on the French border, where there had long been rumours of strange occurrences; healings, miracles, cures; but also of disappearances and unexplained fires. The name of this village was Les Paons. I reproached myself for the unnamed fears that had kept me from this study before, and yet it was with many misgivings that I, one morning in the autumn of 1876, travelled to Les Paons. The coach journey into the Jura took five hours and was all winding, treacherous tracks that caused the horses to struggle and inflicted upon me an unpleasant nausea.

When I finally arrived, I found the village to be traditional in style, with clusters of wooden chalets centred around a cobbled square. It was very quiet and strangely devoid of beauty, lacking the charm that one would expect from such whimsical architecture. Notwithstanding my weak constitution, awkward manner and poor French, still I found the villagers to be hostile and resistant. Not a single person would talk to me about local practices, religious or otherwise. At the time I wondered if their obtuseness was simply due to my being unconversant with local customs, but as I look back now, in the terror of hindsight, I know it was something far more sinister.

Having manifestly failed to engage anyone in conversation, I decided to make my way to the village church, parts of which dated back to the twelfth century. My reasoning was that if the architecture and contents of this church gave me no clues, I could at least pray to God for some inspiration. St Beatus' church stood on a hill at the top of the village, and as I mounted the stepped path towards it I felt eyes, many pairs of eyes, boring into my back, as if the whole village was observing. I knew from my studies that St Beatus had remained a Catholic church, this village having successfully managed to fend off the Reformation. However on closer inspection it appeared to have undergone no less iconoclasm than the Protestant churches that had been so cruelly whitewashed. The medieval gravestones that filled the grassy churchyard surrounding the main building had been left to seed. Many were partially covered by weeds, their engravings obscured by lichen. Any that were cross-shaped had fallen to the ground. A statue of the Virgin Mary had been decapitated and dismembered, while along the church wall, gargoyles and stone reliefs of Biblical figures had been similarly mutilated.

The heavy wooden church door was bolted with an iron padlock which was coated in cobwebs, suggesting that the place had not even been opened, less still attended by a

5

congregation, for a very long time. As I turned away from the church in disappointment, I jumped in fright and clutched at my chest, for in front of me on the pathway stood a huge blue bird with myriad emerald eyes in the tail that it shook at me. A peacock. We stared at each other for some moments before it strutted away.

By now it was late afternoon and, eager to leave this ominous place I decided to give up my quest and return to Geneva. Before enduring that winding journey again, which would no doubt be even more treacherous downhill and in darkness, I decided to steel myself with a drink in the village inn. Almost inevitably the establishment emptied of its few customers when I entered, but I remained steadfast, emboldened by the thought I would soon leave this place never to return. I ordered a mug of ale and when I looked across the bar I noticed that I was not after all the only remaining patron in this establishment. A fellow drinker was propping up the other side of the bar – old, drunk, haggard and unkempt – and whom I strongly believe now to have been a former cleric of the village, hounded from his role. He was staring at me so I slunk away to find a booth, but he immediately followed and joined me, causing me almost to retch from the stench; surely he was a beggar. But he did not ask for money. In a hushed voice so deep as to be almost a growl, he began to tell me a tale. Struggling to follow his accented French, I listened with the strange assertion that all my miserable life had been leading up to this moment; that it was my destiny to hear this tale. The man told me that in the vault of the village church I would find one of two copies that exist of a mysterious book he called the 'Ars Adramelechum.' From the words alone I knew this to be a grimoire, and I also knew the chthonic evil to which it referred. The Art of Adramelech: a spell book to conjure the fire demon Adramelech, and perhaps the key to all the strange events that were reported to have happened in this place.

I noticed that the man could hardly bear to say these words out loud, and after he told me the name of the book he was consumed by a violent coughing, so much so that I feared he may be breathing his last. But he regained his strength, and stared at me for a disconcerting length of time, and he quivered as if agonising over what to do next. Finally, he opened his coat to reveal an iron key which hung on a rope around his neck, telling me it would open a tiny wooden door at the back of the church's nave. He then described to me the sepulchre beneath the church, accessed by moving a stone behind the altar, where I would find the book inside an old chest. He told me never to go to the church, and never to open the book. And then he changed his mind; afflicted by a sudden panic, he gripped me by arm and urged me to take the book, and to destroy it. He took the iron key on its rope from around his neck and pressed it into my hands, looking about him as he did so lest the innkeeper or anyone else should see. Well, dear reader, we all know the perversity of human nature – since Eve took a bite from the apple, since Pandora opened the dreaded box – and from that moment my destiny was set.

My whole life I have been oppressed by a certain timidity of nature, and yet tonight I felt uncommonly courageous. Partly, I own, by liquor, since I had imbibed a not insignificant quantity; but also by some unknown force of temerity that compelled me, that told me nay, I simply must.

I ordered my coachman quietly to return forthwith to Geneva with an empty carriage, uncoupling one horse for myself, which I tied up behind the inn. I waited until nightfall, lurking in the woods outside the village, then crept up to the church, where with much struggling and creaking I was able to use the iron key to open the wooden wicket door into the narthex, exactly as the old man had described. There was just enough moonlight coming through the stained glass windows and the hole in the damaged roof for me to feel my way past the pews to the altar and behind, where the stone moved for me, again just as had been described. At this point I cursed myself for having no oil lamp. I was forced to light a match in order to safely navigate the stone steps that were revealed to me; as one match was extinguished I lit another, and finally reached the floor of a sepulchral chamber beneath the church. It was littered with more broken and dismembered statues; a mass grave of iconoclasm over which I had to clamber, feeling more blasphemous with every step. I was down to my last few matches by the time I found a dust-covered wooden chest. With much heaving and creaking it opened, and there inside lay an object, also covered in dust and cobwebs, but unmistakeably book-shaped. I cleared away some of the debris that covered it, coughing and spluttering as clouds of grey surrounded me. Down to my last match now, I hid the filthy book inside my clothing and stole back to Geneva with much celerity, my precious treasure clutched against my person, my exhausted horse arriving in the early hours.

Of course I had no intention of either sleeping or obeying the old man's instructions to destroy the book. I immediately lit the lamps in my bedroom and began poring over it. The first thing I noticed was its cold, deathly smooth texture, its familiar and yet unfamiliar colour. Yes, it was bound in human skin! I had heard of this custom of anthropodermic bibliopegy, a macabre yet common practice in the seventeenth century. I shuddered at its touch. The second thing I noticed, with some dismay, was that this would be a tedious reading exercise as the text was written in old French. In the end though, this difficulty in reading led me to linger over every word with even more morbid fascination, as I struggled with the meaning of this terrible book.

Although the author offered no clear introduction such as I have done, I was able to deduce – from the signature, date and place, and from textual study – that he was a Catholic priest who around 1650, as the Reformation spread, had been hounded from his parish and fled to the continent, where he travelled for many years. On reaching as far as Damascus, he discovered an ancient Samarian or Phoenician text of unknown authorship but written in Aramaic. He then spent many years studying and translating it. Unable to use the newly-invented printing presses for such a blasphemous book, he wrote it out by hand in old French, making only two copies. He brought them back to his village, which at the time was called Guerillot but was at some point renamed Les

Paons (the significance of this will send a chill down the spine of readers who venture further into the text), and where he was re-installed and became something of a cult leader. His name was Pré Jérome Hugonnet.

As I read on, my eyes grew wider and wider, my heart beat faster and I shuddered continually; never have such terrible words been committed to the page! I should have believed it a hoax, a fiction; a cruel trick by a depraved mind. How could something so appalling be created in the conscience of a mere human?! And yet many of the details, as a theologian I know, can be confirmed by other ancient texts. The Old Testament itself - the Book of Kings no less – tells of a god who demanded the fire sacrifice of children by his people the Sepharvites. Further still, the perfidious contents of this tome, vile as they were, amounted to no less than an oracle into other worlds. What knowledge! Knowledge that opens vast chasms in the mind that leaves you teetering on the brink of your sanity! The Lord God rebuke me if it is not the truth. I ask you again, dear reader, how could something so appalling be created in the mind of a mere human? It could not! For these were the words of demons! Worse than demons – these were words from a place beyond Hell itself!

And so, in this way it was my great misfortune to discover one of these books (the whereabouts of the other is unknown) and to make the first English translation. Here it is consecrated to the reader without partiality, without abridgements, without explanatory notes, other than this here faithful rendition of how it all came to pass. I have tried as much as possible to retain the spirit and character of the old French, but the reader must forgive any errors or discrepancies in tone, for it is most difficult to translate into our modern vernacular.

Finally, dear reader, a warning. A most serious and dire warning. While this work was undertaken in the spirit of academic endeavour and research, I must counsel great caution in the reader's choices beyond this point. I would indeed question the purpose of any reader who takes it upon themselves to turn these pages. My life is now in shadow, and, as the first chapter of the grimoire will point out so presciently, what has been seen cannot be unseen. Everywhere I go, I sense that strangers are lurking, following; my personal effects have often been moved during my absence; I hear noises at night. Several times the charred carcasses of animals, cruelly burned to death, have been left on my doorstep; several times birds have come crashing into my window or down my chimney. My dreams are plagued by unspeakable terrors, so much so that I dread going to sleep and I am by consequence so exhausted I am unable to teach. I have taken to opium to dull my terrors, to whorehouses to avoid the loneliness of my bed. As my rowdy students give up their frivolities and become pillars of society, husbands and fathers, I outstrip them in vice and descend towards my own personal place of annihilation. My sense is decaying, my body ravaged by syphilis and alcohol. And yet I fear less for my mind and body than for my soul, which is wrought upon by the demons whose words I dared to read. I suspect that my end is nigh, in one way or another, and so by sending this text away to England I hope that I may leave some small mark on this world, whether for good or ill.

I realise that my entreaties will be in vain, because I too was counselled, as the reader will be, by the first chapter of this book not to look any further. And of course I could not resist. I did indeed question the morality of my translation, and after much soul-searching I decided that it must be kept for posterity, that to destroy such an ancient and powerful text, no matter how terrible its contents, would be a crime in itself. Choose ye well, exhorts one of the ghastly verses within, and I can but choose the way of truth. And so, dear reader, you must now decide for yourself whether to continue on this journey, or should I say, this descent.

I bid you farewell, and shall remain, eternally, your most humble and obedient servant,

Reverend Doctor William Lovett
Geneva, November 2nd 1879

One

Eliza Bektashi was walking across Crosby's pedestrianised shopping square, as slowly as possible to conserve her energy in the oppressive heat, laden with carrier bags that caused her to list from side to side. Sweat salted her eyes, trickled down her back, and stuck her long sleeves and long skirt clammy against her skin.

She stopped and put down her bags for a moment to catch her breath; there was no rush. She had bought almost everything on the list in the main supermarket, but she couldn't understand why these people didn't buy what they could in the discount stores across the square. There were pounds to be saved every week, and if her employers couldn't be bothered to pocket the difference, then she would. It was not yet midday but already the tables outside the cafes and pub were filling up with customers. Liverpool was in the grip of a June heatwave that showed no signs of abating. The initial stages of British summer euphoria – bare legs, ice creams, barbecues and electric fan sales – had morphed into the inevitable sprinkler wars, newspaper warnings to keep an eye on pensioners – and this too had now waned as a collective lethargy had settled over the city. People were doing the bare minimum and the scent of body odour and knocking off work early had become standard.

Eliza stood for a few moments in the shady part of the square until she had accepted and bathed in her new level of discomfort. Outside the newsagent the local newspaper sandwich board lamented yet another animal burned to death. That made two cats and two dogs in the past month, Crosby pets set on fire in acts of seemingly mindless violence by local thugs, leaving their owners distraught. Eliza shuddered, despite the heat, and fingered for the amulet she usually wore on a necklace, but her neck was bare. She had left it at home. She surreptitiously muttered a prayer, took a deep breath and steeled herself for the blinding sunshine that lay between her and the Homesaver store. But just as she was about to set off, her phone rang; no doubt Madam with something else for her to buy. She fumbled for the phone in her cross-body handbag. The bag's metal clasp had been heated so much by the sun that she could hardly bear to touch it, and she winced as her fingers were scalded. The small piece of metal caught the sun's rays and blinded her as she finally retrieved the phone.

'Hello?'

She could just make out a faint whispering on the line.

'Hello? Hello?'

The whispering became louder but no clearer. It sounded as if there were many voices, perhaps thousands; infinite voices, all whispering in strange tongues that she didn't recognise. The sound was pitchless and insistent and if she didn't know better she would have said that it was not human. Then suddenly there was a searing pain in the pit of her belly, and she screamed and doubled over, clutching at her abdomen. A man moved towards her to try and help, but he stumbled back in terror, falling into an elderly couple behind him, because Eliza was screaming, but instead of noise, flames were licking out of her mouth. Suddenly her entire body was engulfed in fire, as if a switch had been flicked on a gas appliance. She began to run around in circles, in a blind panic, her eyeballs gone now, her arms flailing. She tried to grab at people to help, and they ran from her screaming. Someone came running out of the pub with a fire extinguisher, someone from the bank with another. The foam was unleashed with a hiss but to no avail; if anything the flames rose higher.

The square was empty now except for Eliza's flaming, fading body; people cowered in shop doorways, a few filming on their mobile phones, having decided to commit their enforced voyeurism to public record. Eliza stopped running now, the flames became smaller and were replaced by a pungent black smoke. Her body seemed to disintegrate before people's eyes; flesh burned away and blackened bones crumbled to dust. And then, as quickly as it had appeared, the fire died down and extinguished itself. All that remained was a smouldering pile of white ashes scattered around a pair of feet, which were seemingly untouched. Two severed, cauterised ankles at the top of two charred stumps. The gaudy cheerfulness of the purple-painted toes and pink rubber flip-flops was an affront, an indignity, and yet the only reminder that a human had been there. Every other trace of the woman had vanished. There was an eerie silence for a moment, and then the collective horror took over and the screams began.

***

Detective Inspector Darren Swift and Assistant Chief Fire Officer Matt Adeyemi stood side by side in front of the charred pile of ashes, sweltering in their hazmat suits and masks, both wishing they could pull at their shirt collars underneath. A tent had been placed around the immediate area, trapping inside the smell of burnt human flesh that was so familiar to Matt, as well as another odour, a strange chemical odour that he didn't recognise. In the heat the atmosphere was suffocating. The rest of the square had been cordoned off, whilst community support officers were ushering witnesses into Flo's café which had been commandeered as a makeshift interview room. Inside the tent the fire investigation team were busying themselves; collecting tiny samples of white ash, measuring distances, taking photographs from every angle as they stepped gingerly around the macabre feet and bizarrely untouched shopping bags. This was the first time Darren and Matt had been assigned to the same crime scene.

'Can't say I'm happy to be working with you,' said Matt, unable to take his eyes away from the feet.

'Me neither. What the actual fuck happened here? Give me something – have you ever seen anything like this before?'

'I must admit, there is a really dark correlation with those pet burnings, and the latest incident was only yesterday. But horrible as it is, that's just local scallies, mindless animal cruelty. This weather is making people go mad; it's bringing out the worst in people. There were perpetrators to those animal burnings. Not that we've caught them yet. And there were bodies – the remains of the pets were there to be seen. But this – I have honestly never seen anything like this in me life. There's nothing left. If it wasn't for those feet,' he had to look away and then tear his eyes back to the scene, 'there's no way I would believe it.'

'Sorry if I'm asking stupid questions,' said Darren, rubbing at his forehead. 'But could it have been a cigarette? Cheap flammable clothing? Something to do with this heat? Some sort of protest? I'm just throwing out random ideas. Is it possible that a crime has actually been committed here?'

'With something as weird as this, there's no such thing as stupid questions. What gets me is that there's nothing left. Just those feet. I'm sorry Darren. Forensics will no doubt tell us more. But until then, we can't even decide whose jurisdiction this investigation will be, police or fire.'

The tarpaulin door of the tent unzipped from the outside, and Detective Constable Colette Quinn entered, fiddling with her hazmat suit.

'How are you doing in the café, Colette?'

'Right. The good news is we've got loads of witnesses. Too many – everyone wants to have a go. We've also got plenty of mobile phone footage. The bad news is that we haven't identified her yet, and the videos only capture the second half of what happened. Middle-aged woman, short, heavy build, fair skin, dark hair under a headscarf. Long skirt with flower pattern, long-sleeved top. And the flip-flops we can see. Apparently she was walking from the supermarket when she stopped in the middle of the square, put down her shopping bags and answered her phone. She looked hot and bothered. But I mean, who doesn't at the moment? She was seen to say 'Hello? Hello?' a few times as if she couldn't hear who it was on the phone. Then she panicked, screamed, doubled over and…'

Colette paused and looked at them. 'This next part has been confirmed by at least ten witnesses. Flames came out of her mouth. Like a dragon, one girl said.'

'Fuckin' hell. So nobody knows who she was?'

'No, not yet. Absolutely nothing to identify her in those shopping bags. Any identification would have been in her handbag, which has… gone up in flames.'

'What about flammable items in those shopping bags? Alcohol? Cleaning products?'

'Nope. Just food.'

The three of them stood in a line, observing the scene in silence. Eventually Colette said 'It's like one of those – what are they called? – spontaneous human combustions.'

'Go-ed then Matt,' said Darren, looking across at him. 'Is that a thing? A proper, fire thing?'

'Nope. It's not a thing.'

At that moment the tarpaulin unzipped again and Sergeant Dave Briggs looked in through the canvas flaps. 'Boss. We've got a girl here says she knows who the woman was, but she won't say.'

'What the fuck, Dave. Get her to say.'

'No, honestly, boss, she's proper shaking. I rounded her up from the hairdresser's across the road because she was sat in the window when it happened so she will have seen the whole thing. She's been asking to leave for the past hour. Now says she's changed her mind and doesn't know the woman.'

'Take her down the station then. I'm on me way.'

***

Lacey Collins still had her blonde hair in giant rollers, and she was fiddling incessantly with her nails, mostly in anguish at the ordeal of having witnessed the fire, but with an element of guilty irritation that her manicure hadn't been completed. Her skin was an odd shade of orange, and with the thick dark eyebrows and giant plastic curls piled into a mane, Darren thought she looked like a sort of anthropomorphic lioness. He sat down on the other side of the interview room table. Even now he still found questioning people mildly excruciating, especially in the austere setting of a police station, and he could never decide which persona to take on.

'Right, Lacey, now obviously you've had a traumatic experience today, it must have been horrible to witness that, but we really need your help now. If you know who that lady was, you have to tell us. Think about her family.'

'No, I thought I did, but I made a mistake. Honestly, I gorrit wrong. Can I please go, please? This place is giving me proper creeps, I haven't done anything.'

'Not yet, Lacey, but obstructing our enquiries can be an offence.' He tried a softer tone. 'Look, if you're afraid of something, we can help, we can protect you.'

She looked up.

'How?'

'Nobody will know it was you who identified her. We've interviewed a hundred people today.'

Lacey squirmed a bit more, and then replied.

'Look, I don't know her name. But I know where she worked. In Blundellsands. She was the cleaning lady for Justine Kuper.'

'As in, wife of Liverpool striker, Thomas Kuper?'

'Yeah. Justine is a mate from school. I've been over there loads of times. I was meant to be seeing Justine in town tonight actually.'

She panicked suddenly, and leaned across the table, eyes wide. 'But you promise you won't say it was me what told you?'

'It's confidential, I promise. But what are you afraid of, Lacey?'

'Nothing. Just. Nothing. Can I go now?'

***

The late afternoon heat caused a ripple effect in the haze above the tarmac, as Darren and Colette drove through Blundellsands. Low to the ground, the air appeared pixelated, as if reality was a mirage that could disintegrate at any time. Straggles of schoolchildren were still sloping home, having lingered in the local parks to enjoy the weather. In this wealthy enclave of Crosby, they were all wearing the uniforms of local private schools.

'Right, it's number eight, Sandy Lane,' said Colette, reading off her phone while Darren drove.

'I know,' he said, 'I've been here before, loads of times. Five years ago I did close protection on Thomas Kuper, as weekend work. He got a bit of grief from Everton fans just after he arrived from Switzerland. Couple of burglaries during matches as well.'

'Did you? I wouldn't mind doing close protection on him. I may be a Blue but he is officially gorgeous.'

Sandy Lane was the most prestigious address in Liverpool, and its surrounding area formed one of the so-called footballer belts of the north-west. To live here, these days, was to be a doctor, lawyer, footballer, or criminal; nobody else could possibly afford it. Swift and Quinn drove past a series of detached houses, each one architect-designed and completely different from its neighbours. Many had been built in the Eighties when the area was more affordable, and there was a preponderance of mock Tudor mansions, Gothic follies, Frank Gehry parodies. Some were hidden in their own private forests, behind theatrically winding driveways. Others displayed their huge windows to the world, not that there were many passers-by on this almost-private road, other than the odd jogger or mother with a pram.

It would have been difficult to find number eight, since all the owners preferred their houses to have faux-bucolic names rather than numbers here: The Barn, Willows, Woodlands, The Moorings. But Darren knew exactly where to go, and they pulled up outside an oversized new-build mansion in red brick with a white pillared porch, white-framed windows and a mock-Tudor gabled roof; a mishmash of architectural styles all encircled with gravel behind a wrought-iron gate. They parked on the road outside.

'D'you think he'll be there then?' asked Colette as they

got out of the car.

'Nah. He'll be training. It's the Derby next Saturday isn't it? No, I expect we'll be speaking to the lovely Justine.'

'You just can't keep away from those Killys, can you?'

They rang the buzzer and, having been let through the electric gates, their footsteps crunched along the driveway. The front door opened to reveal Justine Kuper, née Killy. In the identikit world of Liverpool beauties – blonde, long hair, bright-coloured clothes, tanned and groomed to perfection – she had always stood out for being that little bit more beautiful. And for being the niece of notorious crime boss Max Killy. Her mother, Max's sister Val, owned the upmarket clothes shop Foxy Ladies in the centre of town. Expensive handbags were piled high and tracksuits emblazoned with designer logos in this luxury jumble sale, where almost everyone paid with cash. For all these reasons, Justine was Liverpool royalty, to be found in the VIP areas of all the best bars, on the social pages of magazines. She had managed all this without anyone having any sense of her personality or abilities. There was certainly no obvious charm or intelligence on display – her green eyes were somehow both piercing and vacant at the same time, but with a discernible something, that might have been kindness or vulnerability.

Her romance with the Swiss football star Thomas Kuper had been almost inevitable, and everyone in Liverpool knew the story of how they had met, at a fashion show not long after he had been signed by the club. They made an impossibly glamorous couple, and engineered by her mother, Justine was carving a career for herself as a minor celebrity based on nothing at all – a weekly column in a women's magazine, appearances at events in London.

Today Justine was wearing tiny turquoise velour shorts and a matching bikini top. Her gently rounded brown tummy showed only the faintest hints of looseness and stretch marks. Her beautiful face was unusually devoid of make-up and Colette hardly recognised her at first. As with Lacey, her hair was in rollers, and a small baby, perhaps six months old, was clamped to her side.

'Hello Mrs Kuper,' said Darren. 'I'm Detective Inspector Darren Swift and this is Detective Constable Colette Quinn. We're here about an incident that happened in Crosby village today. Have you heard anything about it yet?'

Justine looked even blanker than usual.

'I'm afraid that a woman died, and we have reason to believe that she might have been an employee of yours.'

As Darren was speaking, another woman came to the door and stood alongside Justine. Val Killy was a slightly more haggard version of her daughter, except that her green eyes exuded strength and pride. Her tanned face had been oddly altered by cosmetic procedures, so that it moved little, and only a certain angles, giving her an unreadable, slightly inhuman appearance.

'Mum?' Justine said in a half whisper. 'Where's Eliza?'

Val placed herself slightly in front of her daughter on the step. 'Justine doesn't want to answer any questions. Can I help you at all?'

'Mrs Killy, right? We believe there was a woman who fits the description of the deceased working at this address. And this woman was burned to death today. We need to know who she is.'

Mrs Killy and Justine both raised a hand to their mouths in shock.

'What d'you mean? What happened?'

Colette and Darren looked at each other; how to describe what happened?

'Can we come in?' asked Colette.

They entered a cool, perfectly air-conditioned hallway which led into a large open-plan living and dining area that spanned the length of the house. A sprawling garden lay behind the French windows at the back, and the whole arrangement felt more like Hollywood than Crosby. As the exterior had been a contradiction of architectural styles, so the interior was also a jumble of ideas, with furniture and decoration an unsettling blend of the minimalist and the rococo. A kitchen of clean lines and smooth stone surfaces fought with purple flock wallpaper, plush rugs, ornately framed mirrors and an enormous crystal chandelier that hung precariously over the entire living area.

The four of them sat down awkwardly on long leather sofas that were absurdly low to the ground, causing Colette to topple backwards slightly, and Darren's long legs to bend upwards like a schoolboy. Colette turned to Justine. 'We are still investigating what happened, but there was an unexplained fire in Crosby village and very sadly a woman was caught in it. She died very quickly. Justine, what was your cleaning lady's name?'

'Eliza.'

'Surname?'

Justine looked to her mother. She clearly didn't know Eliza's surname. Val said 'Bektashi.'

Darren continued to address Justine.

'How long has she been working here?'

'Erm, since just before the baby. Just before Christmas. Seven or eight months.'

'Where did you hire her?'

'From an agency.'

'Name of the agency?'

Val looked tight-lipped. Again, Justine looked to her mother.

'Let me guess,' said Darren to Val. 'Was it the agency of your brother Max?'

Val took a deep, irritated breath. 'Look, it's all above board, I can assure yers.'

'So can we take a look at her contract? Can we see a copy of her work permit?'

'I don't have them here. Max could help you with all that.'

Darren turned to Justine. 'Employing someone illegally is an offence, Mrs Kuper.'

'Forget Justine, I'm the employer,' interrupted Val.

'In any case our priority now is formally identifying the remains and contacting her relatives. Can you give us her home address?'

'Here,' said Val. 'She lived here.'

'Do you know anything about her family then? Does she have family in the UK?' Darren was looking pointedly at Justine, because he could see that she was the weaker of the two.

'I don't know,' said Justine. 'To be honest I don't know much about her family. All I know is that she was from… where was it Mum?'

'Albania.'

'Yeah. Albania.'

Colette took out her iPad and showed the women the footage they had taken from the security cameras at the supermarket checkout, documenting what would be the last moments of Eliza's life. 'Is that her?'

'Yeah. Yeah it is.' Justine looked genuinely distraught, and held her baby tighter with both arms, kissing the top of her head. The baby was engrossed in fiddling with Justine's necklace, an infinity-shaped pendant that sparkled with diamonds. Val put her arm around her daughter, cajoling rather than comforting.

'Our Justine's going out soon,' said Val. 'She's got an appearance at—'

'Mum, I'm not going out now. How can I?' She jiggled the baby and tried to engage her in play to distract from her anguish.

'I'll deal with it Justine, it's very sad but it's not your problem.'

Darren felt a curious affinity with Justine. He could barely contain his irritation that this bland beauty had ensnared Thomas Kuper and, yes, if he was honest, stolen him away. And yet they did share this connection to the football star. Darren felt that he and Justine were both somehow floating through life, buoyed by its currents, taking things as they come, successes and failures, perhaps drifting onto paths unexpected to them. He stood up, signalling for Colette to do the same.

'We'll need to search Eliza's living quarters. We'll take some samples of DNA to try and confirm her identity, and go through her things as well. Can you show us please?'

With gloved hands, Darren and Colette searched Eliza's staff quarters which lay in an annexe at the back of the house, collecting Eliza's hairbrush and toothbrush as they went. It was all perfectly well-kept, but spartan and strangely devoid of identifying material. No laptop, photos or utility bills, no passport to be found. Just an envelope of cash in the drawer of her bedside table, on top of which was a Koran, a stack of magazines, and a cheap-looking pewter necklace with a purple semi-precious stone, so large as to be a sort of amulet. A woman who barely existed, at least in Liverpool, with seemingly so little footprint on this world.

'Aha, so she did have a vice, though,' said Darren, peering inside the wardrobe, where a stash of empty vodka and gin bottles were partially hidden behind Eliza's clothes. 'If I had to work for Val Killy I'd probably be driven to drink meself.'

'Look at that. Imagine being so rich that you've got a fuckin' peacock in your garden.'

'You what?' Darren went to join Colette at the window where she was looking out onto the Kupers' garden. An outdoor swimming pool and decking area dominated the part closest to the house, with two used towels draped over loungers where Val and Justine had recently been lying. A single inflatable flamingo floated languidly in the turquoise water. Beyond the pool, there was a large expanse of lawn which swept down to a forested area at the back. Somewhere within this forest was the fence between this and the mansion that bordered it, which Darren knew from his former security work there. Like an apparition, an electric blue bird had emerged from the trees and was stalking across the lawn towards the pool. Its tail, a vast pile of feathers, swept the ground behind it like an emperor's cloak. It stopped in the middle of the lawn and appeared to stare straight at them. As they watched it began to quiver and then in one sudden movement its plumage burst into a full fan, revealing a score of jewel-coloured eyes. Darren and Colette both jumped and grabbed each other, laughing at their fright. The bird paused long enough to allow itself to be admired, then turned on its claws and strutted back towards the forest.

Darren glanced over to the adjacent French windows where Val Killy was also watching the peacock. When her eyes met Darren's she turned away as quickly as the bird had.

The detectives took their leave a few minutes later, informing Val and Justine they would need to come to the police station and provide statements. Val watched them go as they crunched along the driveway towards the electronic gates and their sweltering car.

'What happens now?' asked Colette.

'We'll get on to the Albanian consulate, community groups, Interpol, see if we can find a family member. Hopefully by then we'll have the fire investigation results.'

As they drove away down Sandy Lane, they passed a red Ferrari: Thomas Kuper returning from training.

Darren said, 'Kuper has met his match with Val Killy for a mother-in-law.'

'From what I hear, Kuper can take care of himself.'

'What d'you mean?'

'I've just heard a few things about him, not all good. Anyway speaking of mothers-in-law, how are the wedding plans coming along?' asked Colette.

'Sound, yeah. Well. Matt's mum is dead excited, which is great, but she's got a vision for this to be the gay wedding of the year, and that is so not what I'm after.'

'I can't wait. I've got me dress already. Wedding at Liverpool Carnival? It's perfect.'

'Yeah. It is gonna be amazing.'

'You don't sound anywhere near excited enough, mate.'

'Oh, I am, sorry. It's just… you know me I don't like a big fuss… and it's all happening dead fast, you know. Matt's starting to talk about kids and everything. I still feel like I'm playing house.'

'And what about your family? Any progress?'

'That's a different story, I'm afraid. We haven't spoken about it.'

'Do they even know you're engaged?'

'They will have heard on the grapevine, I'm sure. But the

last time I went over there was nearly two years ago, when I moved back from London. It went so badly I've not tried since.'

'Oh my God, that's insane! So they haven't even met him! You only live round the corner. I didn't realise it had been that long.'

'I know, yeah. I emailed them last year when I passed my detective exams, and I didn't get a reply. Matt thinks I should keep trying, but I just can't keep doing it to myself. Matt's family is mine now. He's got relatives coming out of his ears, and they're all lovely.'

'You know what, your parents are probably just embarrassed at themselves now. Saving face.'

'Maybe. But you'd think that for your only son you'd do a bit of a climb down. Honestly that church, it's evil.'

'Oh yeah, the church is probably telling them all sorts as well. You know, some of what Mainstreet Church does might be illegal. Brainwashing people. Maybe we could get them under hate crimes.'

'What does that say about my upbringing, eh? I spent my whole childhood there.'

'Well, at least the religious brainwashing didn't work on you, mate. I've never met anyone less spiritual than Darren Swift.'

On The Nature Of The Unseeable

Let this be a mortal warning to all that shall attempt the reading of these words herein. Let it be known that he who shall henceforth venture within these pages shall be forever changed.

For it is an undeniable truth that what has been seen cannot be unseen.

The page that is turned cannot be unturned.

Within these pages are contained the secrets of that which lies beyond Hell, in the Infinite Space. Once these secrets are imprinted upon the soul, the path towards annihilation is inevitable, and the reader will drag down many others alongside him.

And so, as the Gorgon turned whomsoever looked upon her to stone, be as Odysseus, who resisted and thus possessed not the horrible secret of her beauty.

As the Sirens called to the sailors to tempt them with fleshly delights, be as the courageous seamen who filled their ears with wax and affixed themselves to the deck with ropes. Their ships were not dashed against the rocks and they passed through danger unscathed.

Be not as Orpheus, who was warned but could not resist turning to look behind him, committing his beloved Eurydice to the underworld for all eternity.

Be not as Pandora; do not open the box!

Temptation is great, and man is weak. Let it be known that even the briefest glimpse of the Infinite Space shall lead the seer and all of his progeny to destruction. O Unhappy Soul, that ye doth consider this path into the abyss!

And so the reader is entreated to leave this book enclosed within its human skin, with pages unturned. To merely touch, with delicate reverence, the silky sheath and to wonder whether its original owner was not skinned alive. For it is said that the power of this tome is magnified eight times if it be swathed in the membranes of one who lived to witness themselves become book. And perhaps what sweeter torture could there be than to suffer oneself to become an article of infinite knowledge?

Let this binding of human skin be a barrier of virgin flesh, never to be desecrated.

1 Ars Adramelechum 2:13

Two

It was almost nine by the time Matt got home that evening to the terraced house he and Darren shared in Waterloo, just a mile away from where Eliza Bektashi had died. Until evidence was found of a crime having been committed, the mystery burning in Crosby would remain the responsibility of the Merseyside Fire and Rescue Service. As Assistant Fire Officer, Matt had been assigned supervision of this case, and was already drowning in paperwork, his least favourite part of the job.

Darren was putting the finishing touches to dinner, which he was serving in their back yard. The windows and door were flung open and Darren had their two electric fans both whirring in the tiny kitchen. They had been eating outside for weeks since the house was unbearably hot.

'You absolute star,' said Matt, kissing him as he squeezed past to take a beer from the fridge. They carried their plates outside and sat at the plastic table on their little patch of parched grass. The sounds from across the garden walls suggested that their neighbours on both sides of the terraced block, all the way down the street, were doing the same. They clinked their beers together.

'Weird day,' Darren offered, before they ate in contemplative silence as seagulls floated languidly above.

Waterloo lay between Crosby and the docks, and behind their back wall the skyline was marked by an assortment of cranes. A battalion of red and white gantries stood ready to load and unload containers, while in the foreground a yellow construction crane lay quiescent, its pendant hook suspended in the stagnant air like a hangman's noose. Darren and Matt had both been drawn inexorably back to this industrial backdrop, only a few streets from where they both grew up. This was where Darren felt he belonged. Not even a childhood tainted by fear and dogma could destroy his love for this city, his need to be here, the draw that it had on him. Sitting here he felt an essential part of the beating heart; a polyp on the teeming coral reef.

Even the strange horror of the day's incident shouldn't have been able to dent their contentment. For the first time in Darren's life he was settled, in his own skin, and with the person he loved. In a place where he was accepted. From his handsome face to his perfect body, from his fierce intelligence to his kindness and bravery, Matt was perfect. Too perfect, so that sometimes it was annoying. He of the endless patience when Darren was struggling with coming out; he of the infinite practicality with the house, always seeing the good in people, always having solutions. Darren was the one with the bad moods, who took his work home, who had a darkness somewhere in his soul that police work only seemed to magnify, and Darren could feel a completely unjustified indignation brewing at his own failings. Perhaps it was Matt's misfortune to have been Darren's first; perhaps it was always going to be like this.

Something ephemeral was bothering Darren now, and it wasn't just the bad dreams that had plagued him since the end of the Andrew Shepherd case. It was something to do with Thomas Kuper. If he was honest with himself, a part of him had jumped at the chance to go to the Kuper house today. And now, a part of him wished he had not gone. Because it had reignited a tiny spark of something that he had pushed to the very recesses of his feelings. Something that had long ago been a bittersweet fantasy and that he had crushed because it was impossible; could never have been. And now, as he clinked beers with his fiancé and breathed in the warm evening air, where the scent of a hundred barbecues mingled with stale sun lotion and sweat, it needled him, scratched at the edge of his happiness. Thomas Kuper reminded him that he was rushing things, repaying Matt's patience with him by doing exactly what he wanted.

Eventually Darren broke the silence and filled Matt in on what he had discovered about Eliza Bektashi.

'Any progress on your end?' he asked.

'We're waiting for analysis on the remains. But at the moment, it's got everyone completely mystified.'

Matt had something else to say, but he was struggling to find the right words, the right tone of nonchalance with which to convey his cynicism.

'Ok. So anyway, listen. One of the reasons I'm late is that I decided to…' He stopped and started again, smiling at himself. 'I looked into Spontaneous Human Combustion for you. I honestly didn't have any other ideas.'

'Go-ed then.' Darren laughed and relaxed. If there was anyone more cynical than him about anything vaguely supernatural, it was Matt.

'Here's the thing. It is a thing. There have been cases. The most recent was in 2010; a death in Ireland was recorded as Spontaneous Human Combustion by the coroner. There have been lots of studies as well, ranging from the insane to the pseudo-scientific. Now, there are some aspects of this case that sound familiar. Spontaneous Human Combustion means incineration of a human body without an apparent external ignition, right? There's a wick effect, fires tend to burn upwards, and burn laterally with difficulty, which explains why objects nearby, like her shopping bags, were relatively undamaged. It's the fat in the body that burns, right, so it's more likely to happen to an obese person, and she was apparently overweight. That also explains the feet left behind in the shoes – they didn't burn properly because they have the least fat in the body. So does our lady fit the profile? If she was an alcoholic then yes, maybe; alcoholism causes ketosis which produces acetone.'

'Acetone?'

'It's a highly inflammable gas, really low flashpoint. It's also miscible with lipids, so it could build up in the body fat and make someone, well, combustible. But anyway if she was Muslim, and a hard worker, it's unlikely she was an alcoholic, right? Worth checking though.'

'Well, she was religious but funnily enough, she may well have been a secret drinker. We found loads of empty bottles in her room.'

'Aha. That could be significant. Anyway, there are other factors too. Severe dehydration increases the likelihood of acetone build up. And who isn't dehydrated right now? Was she wearing cheap flammable clothing? Very possibly, given her socioeconomic background, and it was covering her whole body. But anyway look – the main point is that it's probably rubbish. There's always an external source of ignition. I'm just telling you because I know you like your supernatural shit.'

'Yeah, the exact opposite. Could there have been a spark? A reflection on a mirror or something? I mean, the sun was so strong, and right overhead at that time of day.'

'Can't see how. A slightly – and I mean slightly – more realistic possibility; her phone exploded. You know those faulty phones that have been going off? She was on her phone right before it happened, wasn't she? And they do get mega-hot in this weather. Again, waiting for test results.'

'My God, if it turns out to be that, some mobile phone company is going under. Makes me scared to use mine! What about if she did it to herself? Self-immolation? She was religious, she was illegally employed, may even have been trafficked. So perhaps it was some sort of protest. Except… she was panicking. She didn't act like someone who was doing it on purpose.'

'You would though, wouldn't you?' said Matt. 'Panic. Change your mind. Have you ever seen a clip of those Tibetan monks who set themselves on fire? They always sort of regret it.'

'No I haven't seen a clip of those monks setting themselves on fire. But I know you have, you freak. If you weren't putting out fires, you'd be starting them, honest to God.'

Matt loved fire; the beauty and danger of it; making it, putting it out, understanding it. Ever since he was a little boy, he had planned to be a firefighter. No matter how many times he got promoted through the ranks, he always seemed to be right in the middle of the fray whenever there was a major incident, and there had been a few close calls. Darren couldn't wait for him to take the fire investigator exams he was studying for, to get him out of danger.

They sat in silence for a while longer, drinking their beers, watching the seagulls that ventured closer now, looking for scraps and growing bolder as the heat of the day subsided. Darren couldn't help feeling that it couldn't possibly be a coincidence, Eliza Bektashi being linked to crime boss Max Killy. Clips of the incident's mobile phone footage flashed through his mind; the strange colour of the flames, the way a body suddenly disappeared. A human with flesh and bones and a heart and hair and features, obliterated within seconds to a pile of white ash.

He said, with as much nonchalance as Matt had mustered when he had mentioned Spontaneous Human Combustion, 'I actually know someone who's an expert on religion and death.'

Matt smirked at him. 'Not the nun again?'

'Well yeah. She might know something about, you know, people who burn themselves for religious reasons.'

'I don't think a week has gone by without you mentioning her since Christmas. Why don't you ask her then, get it out of your system?'

'I might do. Just to rule it out, you know.'

***

Dr. Helen Hope was delighted with her new office on, appropriately enough, Hope Street, cradled between the two cathedrals of Liverpool. In the six months since the Andrew Shepherd adventure, things had changed for her very quickly, but it all felt as if it was unfolding as it should. She had a new, tenured position as Senior Lecturer in the Theology Department, a tiny rented flat in Toxteth, not far from the university quarter, and a new project as choir leader at the Liverpool All Angels' Church. Her ten years with the Sisters

31

of Grace were already fading into the memory of a bizarre interlude in her life, although she did miss the kindnesses of some of the Sisters, and of course her beloved green Volkswagen Beetle.

Every morning she ran, almost skipping in her enthusiasm, up the clattering wooden stairs to her third floor office in the university town house. Life was full of promise now, even though in practice little had changed, and without her fellow Sisters she was more alone than before. But then, for ten years she had existed in another dimension, and her forays into the real world had been so brief – a weekly escape to give a university lecture, an occasional visitor to the convent. Now that she was living in the real world, she felt the constant exhilaration of possibility. And this morning she was waiting for an intriguing visitor, after receiving a very unexpected email late the night before.

There was just time to put the kettle on before the bell rang and she buzzed Detective Inspector Darren Swift into the building. She heard his footsteps clattering up the stairwell.

'Just come in, Detective,' she called.

He had expected her to be wearing the severe monochrome habit to which he had become accustomed, and so he hardly recognised her, standing against the window with the morning light illuminating her shape. She wore a summer dress that was demure and knee length but fitted to her body, bare legs and gold strappy sandals that revealed manicured toes. Her black hair hung long and free, framing her make-up free face which was much prettier than he remembered. She looked genuinely pleased to see him and they shook hands warmly.

'Detective, what a nice surprise to see you again.'

'Hello again, Doctor Hope.'

'Call me Helen, please.'

'OK, Darren then.'

The big Edwardian room was light and cool, and although still spartan by most people's standards, Helen was gradually filling it with the paraphernalia of her new life. A huge bookcase dominated one wall, and as Helen poured them some coffee Darren's eyes wandered over Bibles, Korans, works of philosophy, history, a world away from his own.

They sat with their coffees in two corner armchairs which Helen used for her student tutorials.

'So, Darren, I've been wondering what on earth this could be about. I presume it's police business. Is it perhaps about the baby?'

'Baby? Oh, you mean the Andrew Shepherd baby? No, no, nothing like that. But as you know the case is going to trial in the autumn, so we'll no doubt be seeing each other in court.'

'Yes, I can't deny there's something faintly exciting about being a witness on the stand. Although I'm scared at the thought of facing Sister Mary again. And about being cross-examined.'

'You don't have anything to worry about Helen. Not only are you innocent, but you did better detective work than the police.'

They smiled at their shared knowledge of the strange case that had brought them together. One cold morning six months earlier, the body of a young man had been found crucified on Crosby beach, a strange symbol carved into his forehead, and a Bible quotation painted in blood on the cross. This was Darren's first crime scene as a Detective Inspector. His first port of call in the investigation had been Helen's convent, only a mile up the beach, where he had asked for her advice about the religious symbolism at the scene. From that moment their lives had been inextricably linked. The meeting had been tense; Darren unable to disguise his distaste for religion; Helen unable to suppress the curiosity that led to her becoming a suspect herself. Both had conducted their own parallel investigations into prime suspect Andrew Shepherd, a former top geneticist and the tutor of the murdered boy. Fifteen years previously, when he was working on the Human Genome Project, Shepherd believed he had discovered the gene for Original Sin, which he called OS1. Furthermore, he found a marker on this gene which appeared to determine whether an individual was destined for heaven or hell. His theory destroyed his career and, discredited and destitute, he kept his secret close and devoted the rest of his life to finding a 'cure' for reprobation; that is, rescuing humanity from damnation through gene therapy. The murdered boy had been one of his subjects. And he had gone further, impregnating a young woman with a genetically modified embryo which, he believed, would be born without the gene for Original Sin. The baby's mother had met with as grisly an end as the murdered boy, but the baby had survived.

Andrew Shepherd was insane, of course; but he was not the killer. Neither Helen nor Darren realised until it was almost too late that one of the killers had been right under their noses the whole time, within the walls of the convent. The case had been a turning point for both of them. Darren had learned about the sort of detective he wanted to be. Helen had been dragged up from her purgatory back into the real world; had discovered, through fellow suspect Mikko Kristensen, the possibility of love, a future.

Helen shook herself from her reverie. 'Do you know what happened to her? The baby? I often wonder.'

'She's with a foster family, I know that. In Blundellsands actually, a nice family. As for Andrew Shepherd, he's been in and out of a psychiatric unit. It's still not clear whether he'll be deemed fit to give evidence. No, I'm here about an incident that happened in Crosby village yesterday; a woman burnt to death.'

'Oh yes, I read about it in the Echo this morning. How terrible.'

'Well, the thing is...' Now that he was here Darren wasn't really sure what he wanted to ask. 'There's no evidence of foul play yet, and we're exploring various theories while we wait for forensics to come back to us. One of those theories is self-immolation. She was from Albania, a practising Muslim, and there is a possibility that she may have been trafficked. No proper employment records or registration. So I'm wondering if she could have been making some sort of protest.'

'Ah, I see. I do have some knowledge of self-immolation

as a religious practice. I wrote a paper on it once, in the Journal of—'

'Journal of Ecumenical Studies 2012, *A Comparative Analysis of Self-Immolations As Expressions Of Faith.*'

'Wow, you have done your research, Detective.'

'Yeah, I'm getting better at that,' he smiled. They both knew how the Shepherd case had changed him. Only weeks into his promotion to the rank of Detective Inspector, he had gone into the case with a self-conscious cynicism and a determination to follow procedure. Out of his depth, he had clung to the rule book. But Helen had taught him that sometimes the strangest stones are the ones that should be unturned. He had come out of the case open to the possibilities of belief, and determined to follow his hunches.

'Could someone be compelled to do it? To burn themselves alive?' Darren asked. 'This woman answered her mobile phone just before it happened, and the call made her agitated somehow.'

'Compelled to burn oneself alive? Well, there is the practice of suttee; you know, those Indian widows who are made to throw themselves onto their husbands' funeral pyres. But of course that's not relevant here.' She thought for a moment, then began to nod her head and tap her fingers on the coffee mug, trying to remember something. 'There is a religious connection that springs to mind between fire, or at least burning, and telephone calls. But it's the opposite, it's about healing. There are spiritual healers who practise something known as *coupe-feu* – it literally translates as "firewall" – who are said to cure burns, even over the telephone. The practice involves a blend of Catholic prayer and paganism, very specific to the French-speaking part of Switzerland, and what's fascinating is that it's still practised and respected today. Swiss hospitals recommend it apparently as a form of alternative medicine, there's even an app for it. That's what made me think of mobile phones.'

'Switzerland, you say?'

'Yes. Well, it crosses over into the border with France. This was an area in which Catholics had been persecuted after the Reformation, so they clung on to some of their traditional practices, which included healing and folk medicine. And I suppose they adapted them.'

Darren's mind raced. Thomas Kuper was Swiss. Eliza Bektashi, Max Killy, Thomas Kuper, Switzerland — there were dots to be joined here. Somehow. But then he shook himself, because this was ridiculous.

Helen read his mind. 'As you say, Darren, it's irrelevant. Just sprang to mind, that's all. Let me look into self-immolations in Albanian communities for you; perhaps there's something in it. I'd love to help. Do you know anything about this poor lady herself?'

'I can't really tell you anything else about the case I'm afraid. I'm just... casting the net wide I suppose. It's very sad, she didn't seem to have any friends or family here, but we're looking into it.'

They both sighed. Darren looked around the room, not really wanting the conversation to end yet. This woman was such a calming presence, and they were connected in such a strange, inexpressible way.

'So, you're obviously not a nun anymore then.'

'No, I'm a layperson again. I believe I'm the first person to leave the Sisters of Grace alive. So to speak.'

'What does that mean – you renounced your vows?'

'Yes, it was all done very efficiently. Renouncing my vows was a foregone conclusion – I mean, I had broken them all anyway, so it would have been unthinkable to stay. The Andrew Shepherd incident marked a real turning point in my life. I needed something to wake me up. But it was still painful to leave. A sort of Stockholm Syndrome, I suppose, after being at the convent for so long. It was harder on Margaret I think. The Deaconess, you know.'

'Yeah, I met her. She was... formidable.'

'Yes. She had a hold on me for so long. But looking back, she was the one who was vulnerable. I finally realised that she needed me more than I needed her. It's going to be very difficult for them to carry on now with one of their own a murderer; the scandal destroys any hope of future funding.'

'I wouldn't feel too bad. They took ten years of your life, remember.'

'Yes, but it's not just that. Margaret remains convinced about her portents. She was still going on about The Rapture at my renunciation ceremony. She thought it was a sign that something terrible is about to happen.'

'She's not the only one. These are weird times. This bloody heatwave has got to be a sign of something. Climate change, if nothing else.' Looking around the room, he noticed a stack of CDs and recognised the jagged lettering on their spines. Iron Maiden, Metallica, other bands that he had never heard of, some titles that were too jagged even to be readable.

'Are you still in touch with that rocker bloke, Kristensen? If you don't mind me asking.'

Helen smiled. 'Mikko. We do keep in touch, yes. As you can see, I've become rather a fan of his sort of music. Heavy metal, you know. It's quite beautiful once you get used to it. Addictive as well. I'm actually finding it hard to listen to anything else at the moment. But I doubt I will see Mikko any time soon. He's on tour in America at the moment. Our lives are very different, and I like my new situation here, it suits me very well.'

There was a tentative knock on the door; a student was lurking in the corridor for his tutorial, and Helen got up to begin the day's teaching. 'I'll have a think, Darren, and I'll let you know if anything comes up.'

They shook hands again.

'Thanks. It was really nice to see you again,' he said, and he meant it.

On The Personal History
Of Our Lord Adramelech

Let it be known that there was once an angel who fell from heaven. Indeed, there were two angels: Adramelech and Asmadei, though they were clothed in armour of shining diamond, were vanquished by the archangels Uriel and Raphael and fell through the aeons for eight thousand years. And they didst suffer horrific wounds along their fall, their diamonds shattered into a million pieces as they were buffeted against the spiked walls of their purgatory. When they reached Hell, they fell into the inferno where they were repeatedly consumed by tongues of fire; seared, molested, incinerated, only to be reformed each time for their torture to continue over eight thousand years. And Satan watched from his throne, and laughed.

But notwithstanding his glee at their suffering, Satan didst not allow such angels as these to dwell in his dominions. And so, banished even from Hell, they crashed through its fires and found themselves beyond in the Infinite Space, by which time they were maimed with unimaginable ghastliness. They beheld the void; tumbling through swirling vortexes and endless chasms, deafened by the roar of nuclear winds that dragged them through black holes as their lacerated innards trailed behind them. Their skins had been torn from them and their agonies beggared description. For Asmadei, hell would have been as paradise compared to this endless torture. But Adramelech's mind was expanded to the possibilities of infinite power. The fires of hell were nothing compared to the raging torrents of blue and black flames that he witnessed; the blinding light as stars exploded and whole universes were flung into existence before his eyes.

And so their wounds festered in the void for another eight thousand years of torment before they were visited by Satan himself, who said unto them: 'Kneel before me, follow me, and thou shalt be saved from the eternal nothingness of the Infinite Space. Thou shalt have new forms and new positions in the government of Hell. And when the time comes to take up my new Kingdom upon Earth, thou shalt be at my side.'

And so they didst throw themselves upon their knees and proffer loyalty, and Satan lifted them back into Hell and allowed their wounds to be tended by eight thousand tiny demons. And Satan gave them each new forms; Adramelech was given the torso of a man, the head and limbs of a mule, and the tail of a peacock. Adramelech was pleased with this new bodily form and he said unto himself, whilst preening his tail vaingloriously: 'Now I am He of the eight thousand eyes; eight thousand eyes that have seen beyond Hell. I am He that has glimpsed the eternal fire of the Infinite Space. I am He with the strength of the mule, who hath borne the weight of my eight thousand years of suffering. I am He with the body of man, and henceforth my destiny cannot be uncoupled from that of man.'

Adramelech was made Chief of the Samael or jugglers, and rose to become President of the Senate of demons and Chancellor of Hell. For he had pleased Satan with his devotion and personal attentions, as keeper of the dark lord's wardrobe. But Lord Adramelech operated in stealth, for he had in truth no loyalty to Satan. In truth he loathed his humiliation as Satan's plaything, attending his foul throne in the pits of Pandemonium, feigning pleasure at the indescribable tortures of the reprobate, as volcanoes belched fire across a sea of rotting corpses. This was nothing to Adramelech; for his capacity for evil knew not the limits of Hell. He conspired to stay close to his master in order to gain the most intimate knowledge of this same, for his ambition and desire for revenge were far greater than Satan could have imagined. Such were the thoughts of this malignant fiend during his vassalship under Satan.

And this ambition shall grow over eight thousand years

until the time comes for Adramelech to build an army of the faithful on earth, and to banish Satan himself into the Infinite Space, to suffer what he hath suffered, but never to return. When the Lord Adramelech returns, those who have been loyal to him on Earth, those who have been possessed of his secrets, shall be rewarded.

As Satan dressed in the fine clothes that Adramelech laid out for him, admiring himself in the looking glass, our Lord didst look too. Satan had grown fond of his servant and allowed him to share many intimacies. And so Adramelech stood behind Satan and smiled humbly as he smoothed his master's shoulders, keeping these thoughts close:

'I am He, the deepest Hypocrite of them all! Whoever heard of an enemy of both God and Satan? It is I, Lord Adramelech.'

2 Ars Adramelechum 4:1

Three

Under a purple evening sky, a ship was rolling in to the port of Liverpool; a car ferry. The rusty behemoth eased into position and its vast metal doors trundled down their chains like a portcullis. Vehicles began to slowly exit the ramp and disperse; cars first, then trucks. The trucks were stopped one by one by a customs official in a high-vis jacket who wielded a clipboard and hand-held scanning machine. Most had their bar codes checked vigilantly and were then waved on, but the final vehicle to roll off, a non-descript white articulated truck, was not troubled by the scanner. The customs official looked around surreptitiously as the driver descended, disappeared into the crepuscular chaos of the container piles, and was replaced by another who had been lurking nearby. This other driver has an odd limp and was very overweight, causing him to struggle as he climbed into the cab and was waved on.

He exited the port, rumbling over speed bumps, and drove the dirty white truck, which had Spanish license plates but no logo on its side, down the dock road towards the city centre. Vast warehouses on either side formed stark angular outlines against the darkening sky. The driver's mobile phone rang; he fumbled to answer it and put the handset under his chin as he continued turning the wheel.

'Yeah, I'm on me way. Can I call you back? I'm driving. I can't find this address on the satnav but I think I know whereabouts it is. I'll be there in like ten minutes.'

'Where are you now?'

'I'm on the dock road.'

'Right, find a pub, pull over, and go in. Honest. I'm not messing.'

'I've literally just set off! What are you ringing for at this time of night anyway?'

'Stu, will you just do it?'

'Alright, calm down will yer? Here's the Queen Mary, I'll go in for a cheeky one.'

Stuart Killy pulled into a layby opposite the Queen Mary; a well-known truck stop. In the past this area was filled with lively pubs, lap dance clubs, brothels; indeed many establishments provided all three services. A thriving if seedy underworld that supplied the transitory community of sailors, drivers, stevedores. Now only a few were left, the rest boarded up, roofless, or already demolished to make way for regeneration. Stuart was unfamiliar with the truck, and his artificial foot had a poor grip on the brake pedal so that he juddered to a halt, the engine stalling awkwardly. The keys were stuck in the ignition and he had to force them out, unsure if everything was fully switched off. But the headlights were off and the parking brake seemed to be on, so he clambered down from the cab into the hot evening air, easing himself carefully onto his good foot and hoisting up his jeans over the folds of his belly. As he crossed the road to the pub he glanced nervously at the grubby white body of the truck that contained his mysterious cargo. Did he hear noises from inside, perhaps a cry, faint bangs on the inside of the metal? Surely not. Best not to know.

He ambled across the road and into the pub, where he settled at the bar and ordered a pint and some crisps. There was athletics on the big TV screen and this enforced break would not in fact be a problem at all.

Inside the truck, the men had become accustomed to dealing with increasing levels of discomfort, but panic was rising now. Why had they stopped again? There was no more water, the rank smell was unbearable, and a couple of men had gone limp already. One decided to light up a cigarette. They had been told not to, but he needed to calm his nerves. He fumbled in the darkness to retrieve his cigarette packet and lighter. The tiny flame sparked and lit the cigarette tip which crackled comfortingly, providing the faintest illumination to the contours of frightened faces. The smoke wafted throughout the space, seeping towards the engine and the cab.

One man could bear it no longer. He stood up and began banging on the inside of the truck, shouting for help. The others were about to join him when one of them called for calm; his phone was ringing. He had been told to await instructions by phone, and they all crouched silent, expectant. Perhaps they had already arrived at their final destination.

When he answered he could only hear whispering. 'Hello? English?' he shouted, panic rising. But the whispering continued, and he pressed the phone against his ear, straining to hear something he could understand. There was more than one voice; many voices, perhaps infinite voices, all urgent, insistent. Voices that seemed to come from a place beyond darkness, a place beyond terror. And then suddenly, when he could bear the sound no longer, but could not tear himself away, the man dropped the phone and fell on his side, clutching at his abdomen, screaming. His movements were inhuman, as if he were possessed. He writhed and jerked up onto his knees, raised his head to the ceiling and opened his mouth wide, but no scream came out; instead a surge of flames roared from his mouth and set others ablaze. Before the flames were even visible from the outside of the truck, they reached the petrol tank and the vehicle exploded in an enormous inferno that lit up the sky.

Stuart Killy almost choked on his pint; slammed it down onto the bar and hobbled outside, following the other shocked pub clientele. He put his hands on his head and looked around him wildly. Whatever had been in that truck, he was going to be in big trouble. And were those human screams he could hear from inside? Don't think about it, don't think about it. He limped away as quickly as he could, resolving to deposit his phone in the canal on the way home.

Darren and Matt had already drifted off to sleep. Darren slept fitfully; indeed everybody slept fitfully in this heat, but Darren had been plagued by bad dreams, ever since the

43

beginning of the Andrew Shepherd case. He would lie simultaneously sweating and shivering in the early hours, in a state somewhere between awake and asleep. This drifting, this liminal state, somehow made the dreams closer to reality. It was always some variation on the same dream, which usually began in the same way. He was on a path, weaving its way through imprecise surroundings, seemingly rural but with abandoned buildings here and there, some farmhouses and barns, others more incongruous; scaffolded structures, derelict factories, a post-industrial wasteland. The path marked a division between the light and dark halves of the sky, and he was making his way along this centre line towards a black wrought iron gate. Sometimes a hooded figure was standing there, and when he was there he exuded a threatening passivity, a calm certainty that a choice had already been made. Sometimes the hooded figure was absent, but the weathervane, the cockerel weathervane silhouetted against the fiery sky, that was always the pivotal point of the dream. In the dream Darren was gripped by a sense of powerlessness, of having no choice but to go where he was led. And he was cold, so very cold.

He often saw children too; the faces of babies that would laugh and gurgle as they crawled towards him and then metamorphose into horrific beasts that would then shrink and scamper away. Tonight these beasts were bursting into many-coloured flames and emitting piercing inhuman screams as they twisted into horrific contorted shapes and then turned to dust. The sound of screams turned to alarm bells and sirens, and suddenly he was hauled up into reality and realised that Matt was shaking him awake.

'Darren, wake up, you're dreaming again. Look out of the window.'

Darren realised that his phone was ringing, and so was Matt's. Sirens were blaring through the night. Out of their bedroom window, the sky was lit up by a column of flames that illuminated silhouettes in the distance; the spindles of scaffolding, the Liver Bird statues on their high perches.

Early the next morning the temperature was already over twenty degrees on the lower dock road, which had been closed to traffic in both directions for a length of two hundred metres. The upper dock road was consequently in rush hour chaos, but down here there was an eerie quiet. The charred remains of the truck still smouldered and surrounding it a thin veil of black fog hung in the stagnant air, which smelled indecipherably foul. Mysterious dark particles settled on to people's hair, clothes, skin, making them shudder. A lone fire engine remained alongside, flashing its blue lights somewhat plaintively. Fire investigation officers moved gingerly around the site, rapidly overheating in their hazmats and masks.

Superintendent Liz Canter stood behind the cordon, flanked by Darren and Matt. They could hardly bear to look, hardly bear to tear their eyes away.

'Eight bodies in there. I'm going to set up a multi-agency team on this from Canning Place. Darren, I'm not saying the body in Crosby is connected, but I'd like to bring you in on this as the liaison officer between the two incidents. Two death-by-fire incidents within forty-eight hours of each other both involving – we assume – illegal immigrants. It's a weird coincidence. Bring in Colette and anyone else you need from Crosby. We'll convene for our first meeting this afternoon.'

A uniformed officer approached them.

'Ma'am, we've got Stuart Killy. He's at Copy Lane police station.'

'So it was him then. Trouble follows him around. Did he really think an obese truck driver with a limp, known to every police officer on Merseyside, could run away from a scene like this? He's a simple lad, isn't he?'

Darren said 'Yeah, learning difficulties. We go way back, me and Stuart. I'll interview him, Ma'am. That's two fires, and Killys connected to both. I just can't believe he'd get into trouble again so soon after the Shepherd case. Especially something this bad. It must only be weeks since he had an artificial foot fitted; he can't even be licensed to drive.'

'Stuart Killy. We meet again.'

Stuart Killy was waiting in Interview Room One, wearing the same clothes as the night before – oversized Liverpool football shirt and baggy jeans – and biting his nails incessantly. He looked up as Darren walked in and sat down across the table.

'I thought there was a chance you might give it a rest for a few months, but it seems that trouble just follows you around, lad.'

Stuart Killy had had a difficult few years. A loyal getaway driver for his uncle Max since the age of seventeen, he had taken the flack for a robbery gone wrong and spent four years in prison before being released on electronic tag. His greater misfortune, however, was to have lived on the same council estate as Andrew Shepherd. Shepherd convinced the vulnerable Stuart into becoming one of his experiments, beginning the process of altering his genetic code. For Shepherd's enemies this was intolerable; the only solution was to kidnap Stuart and reverse the process. And the only way to kidnap someone wearing an electronic ankle bracelet is to amputate their foot.

Stuart's face and neck flushed with shame, and as he shifted in his seat the smell of body odour and fear wafted towards Darren. He was about to speak when the door opened and, with impeccable timing as always, the suited figure of Mike Fagan entered. Darren was unable to hide his frustration; Fagan was the Killys' solicitor, and had managed to prevent Stuart's uncle, Max Killy, from receiving even a single police caution during his long career as a local mafia boss.

Fagan pulled up a chair next to Stuart, and made a show of laboriously assembling his folders and shuffling his papers, as he said 'Good morning, Detective Inspector. As you know Mr. Killy in his diminished capacity is required by the state to have a specialised representative present at all times, and I'll be acting in that capacity today.'

'Course you will. And you just happen to be his uncle's lawyer as well. Right here we go.' Darren started the tape. 'This interview is being tape recorded and may be given in evidence if your case is brought to trial. I am Detective Inspector Darren Swift. Please state your name and date of birth.'

'Stuart Anthony Killy, 3rd May 1986.'

'Also present is Mr. Killy's solicitor Michael Fagan. Stuart, you were seen on CCTV driving the truck which exploded last night. You then left the scene without identifying yourself. Who hired you to drive that truck? Because according to the Job Centre, you are officially unemployed and claiming disability.'

Stuart opened his mouth to speak, but Fagan whispered to him, 'You don't have to answer that, Stuart.'

Darren sighed. 'Who did you switch with at the port?'

Stuart looked anxiously at Fagan, who shook his head paternally.

'My client will not be answering any questions today.'

'You haven't surrendered your phone, Stuart. Where is it?' Darren persevered, and this time Stuart did speak.

'I've lost it. I must have left it in the pub that night, and someone stole it like.'

'Yeah, that'll be it. We can check your phone records you know. Why did you pull over and go to the pub, just at the right moment before the truck exploded?'

This time Fagan interjected, placing a hand on Stuart's back. 'My client will not be answering any questions today.'

'The address on the truck manifest was fake – it didn't exist. So where were you headed with that truck?'

'As I said, my client will not be answering any questions today.'

'Stuart. Eight people died last night. In a truck you were driving. We can check your phone records. Don't think because you conveniently 'lost' your phone we can't trace them. We can find out who you're working with. Don't you feel—?'

'Mr. Killy is not obliged to answer any questions at this

stage.'

'Leaving the scene of a crime is—'

'There is no evidence that a crime was committed.'

Darren switched off the tape and stood up abruptly, kicking back his chair. 'This is a fuckin' waste of time. I'll have you removed, Fagan.'

But then Stuart, who had been squirming in anguish, finally spoke. 'Detective. I didn't know they were in there. Honest. And I didn't start the fire. Honest. I'm really really sorry. Some bloke in the pub gave me cash to drive the truck. Because I've still got me port access card, like. No questions asked. I'm really sorry. Who were they?' Tears in his eyes, he looked broken.

Stuart Killy was born into the wrong family, thought Darren. *Like me.*

***

Canning Place was the headquarters of Merseyside Police, a 1970s red-brick cuboid designed to echo the dock warehouses that lay across the road, on the waterfront. While its small windows didn't absorb as much heat as the glass-covered Lumina building nearby, the police station had not been designed to withstand a heatwave of this magnitude, and its ageing air-conditioning was proving ineffective. The meeting room was full; every chair around the huge table was taken, and most wall-leaning space was taken too. Darren fiddled uncomfortably with his collar, wishing he was standing nearer the open windows rather than next to the door which kept opening and disturbing him as late-comers trickled in. He looked around the room; there were big guns here, including the Commissioner and Chief Superintendent, and Darren wondered if today had been the best day to wear his trademark fluorescent Nike trainers with his suit. He nodded at Matt who stood on the other side of the room, and Matt winked back. Liz Canter entered and made her way to the front, and a hush fell over the room. Always immaculate in her heels, even she was wilting and had swapped her tailored suit for a sleeveless shift dress, her tanned arms beginning to show the faintest hints of age spots and sagging.

'Right, thank you all for being here at such short notice, as a part of this hastily-assembled task force. You've all been briefed on the terrible tragedy that happened last night...' At this point she switched on the projector which showed an image of the burnt-out truck, mercifully faint against its white background in the sunlight. 'Eight unidentified individuals died in a truck fire on the Lower Dock Road. Almost certainly illegal immigrants, possibly being trafficked. We know they were men. How? Not from their skeletons – the heat of the blaze was so intense as to completely destroy most bone matter. We know from their shoes, which were relatively untouched. As were their feet. Absolutely bizarre that they survived the blast. We're hoping that the fire service can shed some light on that.'

She clicked on to the macabre image of several pairs of men's shoes lying in a pile of grey ash and debris. One individual had been wearing sandals, and his feet were almost untouched inside them, toes visible, the rest of his body gone. There were loud murmurs around the room as Canter continued, raising the volume of her voice.

'The ferry was coming from Spain, but the original source of the truck is currently unknown due to falsified documents including a false manifest. The port official who waved it through is in custody, currently being questioned by Port Police. They will have to explain how this inside job happened. The driver, name of Stuart Killy...' – at this there were groans throughout the room, since everyone knew the Killy family – 'is also currently being questioned. Cause of the fire is as yet unknown. This is going to be a multi-agency operation; we have here representatives from the Fire Service, Interpol, British Transport Police and the National Crime Agency.' There were nods as she gestured around the room.

'It's very hot in here so I'll try and keep it brief, and introduce you to our team leaders. This is Dr. Amira Hassan from the National Crime Agency; she's head of the Modern

Slavery and Human Trafficking Unit for the northwest region, and has come in at very short notice. For many of you this will be new territory, so Amira will give us a briefing so we can understand the context in which we're working here.

Dr. Hassan stood up. 'Thank you, Superintendent. I only wish I could be doing this briefing in less tragic circumstances. Some of you will already have been aware of this, through cases on which you have personally worked; for others this will come as a surprise. But the fact is that human trafficking and slavery is everywhere in the UK. It affects every large town and city, and many places in between.

'Almost 1400 victims were identified last year, and there are currently more than three hundred live police operations ongoing. We also believe this may be the tip of an iceberg, as we don't have reliable data. Another problem is that we don't have decent care plans for victims, so they often fall straight back into the hands of traffickers once they are released. Or, these vulnerable people can fall into destitution, alcoholism, drugs, exploitation.

'Now as for the north-west, occasionally the issue comes above the radar and then disappears again. You all know the story of the Chinese cockle-pickers in 2004, who were swept out with the tide at Morecambe Bay. At least twenty-one people died.'

Canter had been twiddling her pen and stood up again, keen to move on, but Hassan signalled for her to wait.

'Sorry, I know this needs to be a short briefing but I just want to say something specific about this case. We know the bodies in that truck were men. And we know there is a fairly clear gender divide as far as exploitative work goes. Women end up in nail bars, brothels; for men in the UK it is occasionally factory or agricultural work, and often the construction industry. Convoluted supply chains and subcontracting make construction both high-risk for slavery, and difficult to track. Tens of thousands of European migrants work in dangerous conditions without pay or a proper contract and suffer verbal abuse and beatings. And they are often hired by high-profile, seemingly-respectable companies. About one in eight slavery cases in the UK last year involved the construction industry. But much of this industry is in denial that many of its companies are propped up by slave labour. And remember that slavery doesn't just mean unpaid. But it is organised crime. Debt bondage is slavery. A bogus self-employment contract is slavery. Zero-hours contracts, long shifts, dangerous conditions.'

Canter tried to interrupt her again, and this time succeeded.

'We do have to be careful here. The construction industry is at the heart of Liverpool's regeneration, and there's no evidence that exploitative practices are happening here. But thank you, Dr. Hassan, and we will all be working closely with the National Crime Agency as we try to identify the victims and, if we are to assume they were illegal immigrants, their handlers.'

'Over there we have Matthew Adeyemi, Assistant Chief Fire Officer, who will be acting as our liaison with Merseyside Fire and Rescue Service. The fire investigation team will hopefully tell us the cause of the truck fire soon. Matthew, I presume it's too early for any results?'

Matt cleared his throat and stepped forward. 'Too early at the moment, but we should be able to detect very soon whether or not there was an accelerant. The presence of an accelerant would indicate arson. But I have to say that most truck fires are a result of poor maintenance rather than foul play. The feet that didn't burn, I can't explain that yet. Again, an unusual similarity there with the fire in Crosby village.'

Canter continued. 'Interpol will be here tomorrow; they will be looking into ownership of the truck, the origin and destination of the cargo.'

'Over there is Detective Inspector Darren Swift from the Major Incident Team. He's already heading the investigation into the other fire in Crosby village yesterday morning. Detective Inspector Swift is experienced in handling the Killys, and will be looking into any connections between the two fires, assisted by manpower from Crosby Police Station. It's hard to see what those connections could be, but it's such a strange coincidence, and at this stage, everything is on the table. Two deaths by fire within forty-eight hours, both with Killy connections.'

Darren breathed a sigh of relief. Being in a cog in the wheel of a large team, headed by his mentor Superintendent Canter, reporting to someone else, in a supporting role; this was far more his thing. The Andrew Shepherd murders had been his first case as a detective inspector, and he was the first to admit that he had been out of his depth. But he had scraped through with a result, and a wealth of experience, plus a good relationship with Crosby Police Station. He was comfortable with DC Colette Quinn and Sergeant Dave Briggs, as well as Dave's sidekick Sergeant James 'Baz' Barry. He knew they'd be up for the challenge of a secondment to Canning Place, and he'd already called them in. Despite the little romantic misunderstanding between them, Darren and Colette made a great team, and since Dave had proved himself at the end of the Shepherd case – indeed, he had ultimately provided the crucial step that led them to the killer - Darren saw the young sergeant as something of a protégé. But this case, he thought, could turn out to be even more tangled and complex than the Shepherd case. Unravelling the layers of Killy family loyalties was going to be a huge challenge, and Darren thought this could be his chance to finally nail Max Killy, the criminal who had been his nemesis since his time in the Drugs Squad.

By the time the meeting ended it was late, but Darren, Colette and Dave were filled with adrenaline and they convened in the office area they had been assigned, surrounded by beige plasterboards. Darren started as he always did; with a diagram on the incident board. Eliza Bektashi on the far left, the truck on the far right, and Max Killy in the middle. Max was connected to Eliza via his sister Val, and to the truck via his nephew Stuart.

'Now let's face it,' he said, wagging his marker pen in front of the whiteboard, 'neither of these incidents were accidents. Why? Firstly, because how can anyone pretend it's just a coincidence that the Killys are connected to both. And secondly, because that truck manifest had a non-existent address on it. But Stuart Killy was going somewhere. And long before he arrived at this non-existent address he received a phone call, pulled over and got out, conveniently before the truck exploded.'

'Fair enough, boss, it's well suspicious, but why? I mean, why would anyone involved in a dark business such as people trafficking want to draw attention to themselves?'

'To frame someone else? Maybe there are rival groups competing for territory, and horrible as it is to think about, they could be using people as bait. When Shawn Forrest turned on the underworld he all but destroyed most of the criminal enterprises in the city. He levelled the playing field, and it's a free-for-all out there at the moment; there are foreign gangs coming in that we just can't keep up with. And maybe someone, like Max Killy, has found an opportunity to take his revenge.' Shawn Forrest was the former crime boss, now successful property developer, who had engineered his release from prison by exposing the secrets of just about every drug-related activity in the city. His revelations had led to multiple arrests and had been a huge coup for Merseyside Police. Max Killy had managed to evade justice, but his empire had been decimated.

'But then,' asked Colette, 'why would Max use his own nephew?'

'Maybe Stuart was the only person he thought he could trust, plus he had a haulage license to enter the port. He was already a driver. The mistake Max made was thinking that Stuart was intelligent enough to get away. And he wasn't.'

Darren knew he was missing something, or perhaps that he was jumping the gun, and his team looked unconvinced. This was an odd remit they'd been given.

'So where do we start?' asked Colette. 'We'll be waiting a while on analysis from either of the fires.'

'If we can find hard evidence that proves Max hired Eliza, or that he owned that truck, we've got him. So let's work on those two strands; let's build up two pictures, of Max and

Eliza, and see how they link. Colette, start tomorrow morning by building up a profile of his so-called legitimate business interests. Since last year, when he became an informant himself, it's actually weird how clean he is. I say clean, I mean he's got cash businesses coming out of his ears – but who doesn't around here.'

'Dave and Baz, I want you to try and find out who knew Eliza Bektashi. Look into the local Albanian community – she must have known someone. What reason would she have to die? What did she know? I'm going to pay a visit to our friend Max Killy tomorrow morning, and we'll take it from there. Questions?'

'Boss,' asked Colette. 'That's all fine, I can get stuck in to his various businesses. But how are we going to build up the full picture? If all the businesses are in cash and no-one ever talks.'

'Well, I do have an idea. You're right that going undercover against the Killys is almost impossible. But on Saturday night it's the opening of the Lumina Building. The jewel in the crown of Liverpool's transformation, or whatever they're saying about it. Shawn Forrest's redemption. The great and the good of the city are all going to be there, and that means a Killy-fest, plus everyone in between.'

'Are you going to go down there then?' asked Dave.

'I can't, and neither can Colette. Too many of them know our faces. So Dave and Baz, you're up. Colette, your job is to get these two on the VIP list for that party. And Dave – do your research. Make sure you know who's going to be there and what they look like. I want to know who talks to who. It's a weird one, but we've got a real chance here. To get Max Killy for good.'

Colette raised her eyebrows at him, and he knew what she was thinking. Those eyebrows of hers were like the voice of his conscience. To stay on remit. But the opportunity to finally get some hard evidence against Max Killy was too good to resist.

On The Journey Of The Sepharvites of Sepharvaim

It is told that there was a great and mysterious people in the region of ancient Samaria. At some time they were wrested from their homes by those who refused to countenance their traditions, and who wilfully misunderstood them, in order to take advantage of their land and resources. The Sepharvites were forced to make a long migration across deserts and mountains. When they were so parched and weary that they could barely continue, they were suddenly drawn to a great fire in the distance that they thought was perhaps a mirage. As they approached, they saw that this was no ordinary fire; it burned brighter than the sun and they were forced to shield their eyes and their children.

And behold, the Lord Adramelech appeared to them, and said unto them in a voice like the roar of thunder:

'Who is He that hath knowledge greater than both God and Satan? It is I, Lord Adramelech! Know that both God and Satan are mine enemies. I too was wrested from my home; I too know great suffering. But I also know this: forgiveness is weakness; revenge is all; and power begets power. Look upon this fire! Look upon it!' And he revealed to them the secret of the flames beyond Hell. And he said, 'If thou dost kneel before me, thou shalt see it in thine eyes! Thou shalt see it in thine eyes that shall be as windows beyond Hell.'

They looked, shielding their eyes, and this fire revealed to them great and terrible things, beyond knowledge itself. And they were sorely afraid and they bowed down before him. And he said 'Arise, o my people, you who have knowledge of the flames beyond Hell. Do not come unto me, for I shall come unto you. You shall be my army upon Earth, and when the time is right, we shall rule this Earth, with its Heaven and Hell, together. But know that the time will not be short; eight thousand years shall be the struggle! And so I command you to write down all that you have heard, and all that you have learnt, and commit it to scripture that must be bound in human flesh. This flesh must be skinned from a live virgin, male or female it matters not, and this virgin must watch as their bodily membranes are committed to posterity, and their screams shall be infused within the pages. Then, O Sepharvites, keep the scripture safe so that your descendants and their descendants after them shall know of the Lord Adramelech.'

And it came to pass that the Sepharvites after them were scattered and found no new homeland. They were much changed by this knowledge and almost all came to perish. Yet a small number among them, those with true flames in their hearts, obeyed their Lord Adramelech by recording these things for posterity, and binding them as He had instructed as they listened to the screams of virgins. And they kept the knowledge He had imparted to them, a fire burning close to their hearts. They hid in plain sight, choosing all manner of faiths to conceal their true loyalty. They became skilled in the craft of artifice and they dwelled in the realms of duplicity.

7 Ars Adramelechum 13:1

Four

'Detective? I mean, Darren?'

'Speakin'?' Darren was sitting at his kitchen table going through paperwork and emails when Helen rang. It was ten-thirty in the evening and still not quite dark.

'It's Helen Hope. I hope you don't mind me calling so late.'

'No problem, I'm still up working. What can I do you for?'

'I'm probably just meddling again, you know me, but after you left yesterday morning, I couldn't help thinking about those Swiss mystical healers, you know, the practice of coupe-feu, and about what you said. And I wondered, if you can pray to cure burns, what if you could do the opposite: what if you could pray for fire? And then, if you can pray to heal someone, what if you could pray to cause objective harm? Because there are saints that are said to be able to put out fire and cure burns, and conversely, there are demons that can supposedly control fire. I must admit that after I met Mikko I did rather get into reading about demons, it's enormous fun.'

Helen was in the reading room at Liverpool Library, seated at her favourite table and whispering into the mobile phone she was still learning how to use properly. It was late on a Friday night and the place was almost deserted. It was also mercifully cool within the stone walls of this imposing Georgian dome. She was in her element here, surrounded by books and on a research trail. When she was in the zone, immersed in a project, she could sit for hours, forgetting to eat or drink, only realising at library closing time that her buttocks, neck and back were stiff and aching from perching on a wooden chair, and that she was desperate to pee. Tonight she had laid out before her at the oak desk an array of bizarre texts, many of which were quite the opposite of those she usually studied. To one side she had amassed a collection of obscure medieval magic books and spell books, many with enticingly mysterious Latin names: *Ars Goetia, Wierus' Pseudomonarchia daemonum, Compendium Maleficarum, Black Books of Elverum.* Some of them she hardly dared to open since they seemed so blasphemous: *The Lesser Key of Solomon, The Satanic Mass,* the works of Aleister Crowley. She had already heard of Aleister Crowley; in fact it was Mikko who had told her all about him. Crowley was an English occultist who had founded his own religion called Thelema which, according to Mikko, had had an important influence on heavy metal. On Helen's other side were academic works about religious healers, European witchcraft, Swiss Catholicism, pagan traditional medicine. These she felt more familiar with, and this academic pile of books grounded her in the idea that she was doing something studious.

There was bound to be a lecture or even an academic paper in here somewhere, she smiled to herself. Something to justify her meddling again in police affairs. And after all, Darren had asked her for advice. Although she had the library to herself, she spoke with hushed tones into the mobile phone that she still found such a novelty.

'So Darren, are you still with me? Good. Now as promised I looked into your question about self-immolation, and I'm afraid I didn't find anything that relates specifically to either Islam or to Albanian culture. It tends to be something practised in East Asia, by Hindu and Buddhist cultures. However, I did get rather side-tracked by those Swiss healers I mentioned – you know, the ones that can cure burns. I read in the newspaper that witnesses saw flames coming out of that poor woman's mouth, and it did make me think of that passage in the Book of James, "the tongue is set on fire by hell." So I did rather wonder whether the healing process could be reversed, as you suggested, so to speak. I'm rambling aren't I? I do get over-excited.'

'No, no, you're fine, I'm listening!' Darren covered the phone with his hand to mouth to Matt: 'It's just one of my sources. She's going off on one. You go to bed, I'll lock up.'

'So,' continued Helen, 'it turns out that this practice of coupe-feu that I told you about, well, it's still extraordinarily prevalent in the Jura region of Switzerland, and it is commonly done over the phone. If anything there's been a resurgence in this sort of traditional medicine, or white magic. But there has also been a resurgence in... well, the opposite. Black magic. There was a scandal in the local press in Switzerland about five years ago. There was a particular village near Geneva where a barn full of cows burned to the ground.'

Darren sat up in his chair. 'Burning cows, did you say?'

He thought of the cats and dogs that had been burned to death in Crosby, just this month.

'When the police investigated they found this village cult, and there were claims of witches, animal sacrifices. Of course the locals said the cows were diseased and had to be culled. Probably all rumours and nonsense.'

'What was the name of the village?'

'Les Paons.'

Darren quickly typed, *Where was Thomas Kuper born?* into his search engine, and the answer came up immediately. *Les Paons.*

The lights were going off in the library and the librarian was hovering, jangling keys.

'I'll have to go now, Darren,' said Helen. 'Sorry to have bothered you. Silly really. But thank you for putting me on to this. You know, I've decided to pop over to Geneva and look further into this coupe-feu practice; there's definitely an academic paper in there somewhere. And besides, Geneva is the home of Calvinism and of course I was a Calvinist nun for so long, I really do owe the place a visit! Anyway, there you go. My new-found spontaneity. Good luck with the case.'

'Goodnight, Helen. Thanks for calling.'

Darren sat motionless for a while, lost in thought. *Eliza Bektashi, Max Killy, Thomas Kuper, Helen Hope...* There were connections there, lying just out of reach. Something was stirring, something he could neither define nor grasp, but which was compelling him down a strange path which he felt sure was somehow connected to the case. Even at this late hour there was no respite from the stifling air, and he could hardly remember what it was like to be cold. The Crosby burnings were taking their place amongst the host of bizarre stories from the heatwave that gripped Europe, and everything seemed to be veering towards a point of unreality, as if nothing mattered any more. His reality was a prism; a crystal that when turned in the sunlight polarised into infinite rays of possibilities. And perhaps somewhere within, beneath the veneer of morals and correctness, there lay the truth, and perhaps it was far stranger than anyone could imagine. Darren's laptop was still open at the Thomas Kuper search, so that a row of images of the footballer lay across the top of his screen; Kuper grimacing as he lunged to kick the ball; celebrating a goal with his arms aloft; posing at a black tie event with Justine. Matt had moved noiselessly into the kitchen to get a glass of water, and he snatched a brief look at the screen before Darren snapped it shut, blinking himself into a smile at his fiancé.

***

Six-thirty am was the only time to jog in this weather. Usually Darren would head straight down to the beach and run along the sands towards Formby, but today he made a short detour towards the docks. The roads were still quiet so there was no roar of traffic from the flyover as he ran along the edge of the wire fence that separated the huge container area of the Port of Liverpool from Crosby Road South. As he ran past, he looked at the colourful contents of the port with as much fascination as he had when he was a child, and its visual riches buoyed him with energy. He loved the logistical, geometrical complexity of it, the way everything had its place. The bizarre, alien-like rusty machines that did who knows what; the treasures to be discovered and shipped on abroad. Giant ships would ease into their channels where no water could be seen, as if they had beached themselves like whales. They would appear and disappear before you knew it, hundreds of thousands of tonnes moved on and off by a ghost army.

As Darren marked the perimeter today he was looking for something specific. The hole in the wire fence where the mystery driver had disappeared. This had already been located by the Port Police, and here it was, still cordoned off despite the forensics having been completed. The driver had weaved his way amongst the containers, caught by a couple of security cameras along the way, and then escaped in the one weak spot on the perimeter that was not covered by cameras. Either he or an accomplice had severed the wire with cutters, and then he had simply vanished into thin air. This was someone who knew what he was doing, who had been carefully briefed about the detailed schematics of the port and beyond.

Darren stood and looked around him for inspiration, catching his breath. It wasn't within his remit to chase down this driver – that was for the Port Police – but he was sure it could be done, and in any case, he thought, the Port Police would be far too busy saving face after this disastrous lapse in security. Where did the driver go? Did he run underneath the flyover into the housing estates beyond? Was he collected by a waiting vehicle? Darren was beginning to be frustrated now that he didn't have a more central role in this case. He was also beginning to wonder if Canter had side-lined him on purpose. Perhaps he wasn't her golden boy after all, but an annoyance who had been promoted too soon. The old self doubts were creeping back, and he tried to shake them away.

When he turned back to the wire fence, he jumped in fright, because a flock of seagulls, perhaps eight of them, had landed noiselessly on top of the fence and perched in a line, motionless and staring at him. They were enormous birds, and he wondered if they might even be albatrosses, so gaudy and out of place did they look in their ungainly size. For a moment he was mesmerised by them, and then jumped again as one of them screeched and they all took flight. They circled low above his head for a few moments, their enormous wingspans placing him in shadow and disorienting him, before they took off away from the sea towards the city. Normally seagulls flying inland were an indication of bad weather approaching, but in this bizarre new microclimate, who knew what it signalled.

Darren ran back through Waterloo, but still didn't head towards the sands. Today he turned right down Bank View, known as 'sunbed strip'. This long road parallel to the beach was lined with large Edwardian terraced and semi-detached houses, once the grand residences of merchant seamen. Now these buildings were either divided into apartments or fronted as commercial units, and the street was populated by an absurd number of cash businesses – nail bars, tanning salons, hairdressers, repair shops. Some of them, such as the costume hire shop and the off licence, were local stalwarts that had been there since Darren was a child. Other units had an almost constantly revolving ownership and signage.

With its everyday glamour Liverpool was one of the places where this number of aesthetic businesses could almost – almost – be credible. It was the expensive-looking ones that aroused the most suspicion. The police mostly turned a blind eye to these businesses, but now as Darren jogged he wondered whether any of these establishments across Liverpool contained trafficked people, possibly there against their will. He wondered whether behind the doors of these once-grand houses, most of which were council conversions now, there could be prostitutes, slave labourers. Dr. Hassan's word rang in his ears as he imagined the many layers of misery that were to be uncovered even in a city of hope.

Again Darren had the sense of a world fraying at the edges. The pale, misty quality of the morning light made everything seem as a mirage, a veneer of normality. That if he peeled away the layers, scratched the surface even a little, something else would be revealed, possibly infinitely more horrible. As with the climate change that had no doubt caused this infernal heatwave, perhaps denial as a way of life was causing people to drift into all manner of horrors.

Darren told himself he was simply nervous about visiting Max Killy later that morning. Max was a highly unnerving presence at the best of times, and Darren had had many dealings with him during his year on the Vice Squad. Max had not had anything to do with the Shepherd case in the end, and he was furious at having been dragged into it. This time though, Darren thought there was no question that Killy was involved somehow, was maybe even behind it. But there was no evidence, only coincidence and hearsay. And so the manner in which Darren had handled this encounter could determine everything. He must keep his cool and outsmart Max.

Before heading home he decided to run across the main road into Litherland, the territory of Max Killy, as if to mark it out for himself. He would never have told Killy, but Darren had grown up on the same street as Litherland Muscle Gym, Max's headquarters. The gym itself hadn't been there when Darren was a child; then it was just a derelict first-floor factory unit; but Darren had been a regular customer to the retail outlets underneath, before they themselves had closed down: the newsagent, the launderette, the fish-and-chip shop. He would stand across from the building with his parents while they waited for the bus that took them to Mainstreet Church on the other side of the city.

The Mainstreet Church where he had been forced to waste so many hours of his childhood, worshipping a God for whom he could feel nothing except fear, and whom he was sure would hate him once He discovered Darren's secret; the secret of who Darren loved. Perhaps He already knew. And as Darren got older he was inculcated with, not only self-loathing, but the absolute necessity of changing, curing himself. Perhaps he couldn't help associating Max's territory with the bitterness he felt about his childhood. The bitterness he felt about his parents. There was no contact with them now. He had reached out to them after he had returned from

London, when his efforts to start a new life had resulted in a homophobic attack that had ended his career with the Met, when he had never felt more alone. But his suffering elicited from them only 'We told you so.' After he qualified as a detective and made the local papers in Liverpool: nothing. Darren had lost the will to keep trying with them, but he often ran past the house; hoping and fearing that there would be some glimpse of them, or even a chance encounter. He thought about Helen and how she had also lost her family to misplaced guilt and shame following the death of her brother. The difference with Helen was that she believed in this God that had stolen so many years of her life and caused her so much pain.

***

Darren and Colette climbed the stairs of Litherland Muscle Gym, taking in the now-familiar musty smell of dust, PVC and sweat, the sound of pummelling and heavy breathing. They entered to find Max Killy bench pressing in an otherwise empty gym, watched over as usual by his silent and beautiful personal trainer. Both were wearing the tiniest lycra gym gear, although there was no longer any surprise in seeing expanses of flesh on display in this weather. Darren and Colette stood awkwardly awaiting his attention. They knew the routine.

'Hullo, Darren.' said Max without stopping his exercises or looking in their direction. 'I expected the bizzies sooner to be honest. I thought they'd be sending the big guns though. How's Canter?' He finally placed down the barbell and sat up.

'Me old mate Dazza. Nice trainees,' he nodded at Darren's footwear. He then turned to Colette, making a point of looking her up and down. 'Hullo, queen.' He was handed a towel and a bottle of water by the gym girl, and took a theatrically long time to compose himself, wiping the towel over the orange folds of his neck, the tattooed bulges of his body. His short stature accentuated the broad shoulders under which his massive biceps would not fit next to his sides and caused his arms to stick out in a top-heavy cartoon stance. Finally he said, 'So what can I do you for?'

'Come on, Max,' said Darren. 'I wanted to bring you in to the station, but apparently you've still got friends in high places.'

'You've got it the wrong way round, lad. I'm the friend in high places.'

Darren stepped forward. He had no patience for Max's games today.

'Eliza Bektashi, burned to death, illegal immigrant, and we both know she came through your,' he put up his fingers to indicate inverted commas, 'employment agency. Eight unknown illegal immigrants, who possibly will never be identified. In a truck driven by your nephew. Who conveniently got out of the truck just at the right moment. How d'you feel about that, Max?'

'It's Mr. Killy to you, lad.'

'How d'you feel about that, Mr. Killy?'

Darren could sense movement behind him, and glanced back to see Mike Fagan standing up from behind his desk in the glass-fronted gym office, and moving towards them. Max signalled for Fagan to remain where he was, and then stepped up to Darren. He was several inches shorter than Darren, but made up for the height difference by invading his personal space to within millimetres of his body.

'Listen, yous. These days I've got massage parlours, nail salons, sunbeds, and this gym. Those were eight men who died in that truck. Men. What would I want with eight men? And Stuart doesn't work for me anymore, I've told you that.'

'Come on.'

'Never mind come on. You come on. Who needs cheap male workers? Think about it! The construction business! And I'm not in it, I've been blackballed all over the place. You wanna be looking at Forrest Group.'

'Shawn Forrest? Everyone knows he's gone straight. He's a city councillor now. And the word is that you and others like you are jostling for position to take his place in the underworld.'

'My arse he's gone straight. Anyway, how many straight city councillors do you know? They're all as bent as you. No offence, like. Big supporter of the gay community, me.' Max suddenly laughed manically. 'Hey, Mike, listen to this. Darren thinks Forrest has gone straight.' On cue Fagan and the gym girl joined in with his laughter.

Darren and Colette shuffled on their feet, looked at the floor, looked out of the window, tried to look inscrutable. Behind them two youths in boxing gear arrived at the doorway, but on seeing the police they quickly left, Max waving them away as he continued, on a roll now:

'Take a look at that monstrosity Forrest has built on the docks. Lumina.' He spat out the word in disgust. 'How d'you think he's going to fill those apartments? How d'you think he's going to pay for that bombsite opposite?' Max was referring to Lumina 2, the sister building across the road from Lumina, which was still a shell of concrete encased in scaffolding, watched over by the Liver Birds. 'Listen, sunshine, look elsewhere. I am small fuckin' fry now. Look closer to the establishment, the powers that be. Private sector investment? My arse. What name do you see plastered all over the building sites? Is it Killy? Is it fuck. Forrest Construction, everywhere you go. If anyone's gone straight, it's the Killys. *Legitimate businesses'*, he over-pronounced. 'That's what we do now. Have you been round here sniffing for drugs recently? No you fuckin' haven't. Why not? *Because there are none.* There's a new breed in town.' He said the word "breed" with gnashed teeth, nodding his head forward violently towards Darren so that it was almost a head-butt, so that Darren could feel the spit on his face, could taste his contempt.

Killy did have a point. He was of the old guard, the traditional gangsters who in the Sixties and Seventies had plundered the docks with abandon, taking their pick and filling vast warehouses with stolen goods. By the Eighties and Nineties the port was still riddled with leaks to be exploited, but the city was becoming flooded with drugs and consequently a new generation of criminal organisations.

Max saw himself as old school; he was also a devout Catholic and initially wanted nothing to do with the drug trade that didn't form part of his own personal moral code. But port and warehouse security technology had become insurmountable, the risks of burglary were too great, and the lure of drug money irresistible. So Max eventually threw in his lot with the drug barons and for a while became the most successful and feared of them all, capitalising on his network of logistics and weapons.

And then things moved on again. The drugs became harder, the routes changed, the contacts changed, and the levels of brutality and array of weapons were too much even for Max's scruples. He was overtaken by a new generation, the likes of Shawn Forrest, and then things came full circle and he was destroyed from within. His only chance of survival was becoming an informant himself, and he had developed a working relationship with Superintendent Canter that caused her no end of headaches. But Max had reached the end of his usefulness to the police now, and Darren knew he felt adrift. Darren also had to admit that he shared some of Max's suspicions about Shawn Forrest, unpopular as that opinion was. Could someone really change that much? In any case, this was about the Killys, not Forrest, and Darren didn't believe for a second that Max had gone down the route of legitimate business,

Colette decided to try. 'Can we sit down somewhere, Mr. Killy? We'd like to ask you some more about Eliza Bektashi.'

'Ah, she speaks. Can you see anywhere to sit? Sit here, queen.' He gestured to the sweaty padded bench where he his bare back had just been lying. 'No? Don't fancy it?'

Colette rolled her eyes. 'Did you provide Eliza Bektashi for your sister to employ as a housekeeper?'

'No. I've never heard of the woman! Horrible, what happened to her. I wouldn't wish it on me worst enemy. But Val just found her off of one of those noticeboards in the post office, cash in hand, dead easy.'

'So you do know how she hired Eliza Bektashi?'

'Only because she phoned me last night, in a panic like,

wanting advice. But I had nothing for her. Val may be me sister, but she's too busy making her moronic daughter into a celebrity to be of any use to me.'

Darren and Colette looked at each other. Darren opened his mouth to ask another question, but was interrupted by Fagan, who had sidled out of the office onto the gym floor.

'Mr. Killy has a business meeting now, so if that's all, detectives…'

Darren and Colette left the gym deflated. As they descended the narrow stairwell, they brushed past a group of burly men on their way in. The men wore shiny suits and carried briefcases, and looked as if they were about to do anything but have a gym workout.

'He sold his sister down the river without a second thought, didn't he,' said Darren, raising his eyebrows at Colette as they looked back at the men.

'It could be true though. Val could have hired Eliza independently, through the small ads. Then lied about it to us, hoping that Max would step in and save her.'

'Yes, it's possible. One of them is lying, anyway,' said Darren, as they got into the car. 'We'll get him one day. On something. While we're trying to get answers on Eliza, let's look deeper into his finances. I can't believe he hasn't been tempted by match-fixing, with a nephew-in-law like that to threaten. He has a direct line to Thomas Kuper. Eliza could have been some sort of warning.'

'Oh my god, really? I know match-fixing exists, but I thought it was more in the lower leagues. Also I would have thought there was some sort of moral code about it around here.'

'Yeah, well everyone has a moral code until they get an offer they can't refuse. Max Killy had a moral code about drug-dealing, until he decided it was too profitable to ignore, and then he was all over it. I'm going to look into putting a watch on the gym.'

'I'm not sure you'll get the budget for that, boss, even if we had grounds. Our unit is on a shoe-string, I mean, our research team is Dave and Baz, d'you know what I mean?'

On Sacrifice

It is told that the Sepharvites didst sacrifice their children in the fire to Adramelech, for this is what their Lord demanded. He said unto them in the desert: 'Cast off all feelings of love and compassion, for therein lies weakness. There is no love, there is only hatred. There is no kindness, there is only cruelty. I have no need of an heir since I am eternal. Destroy your own heirs and I shall make you immortal in your turn. Do this in my name.'

And so the Sepharvites didst commit themselves to this promise. They fashioned a great vessel of burnished bronze, and in the middle stood an exalted bronze idol of their Lord. His human hands were extended with palms up, arms sloping down towards the flames, and his face struck the most ecstatic fear into their hearts. They lit the furnace so that the vessel was a gaping pit of fire, the flames licking over their effigy's hooves and up towards the fur of his crotch and belly.

But when the moment came, they were sore afraid, and wondered if this was a test. And then suddenly a voice appeared from the mouth of the bronze idol:

'God was weak, for he stopped Abraham from sacrificing Isaac at the last moment on Mount Moriah. Didst thou think that I would be weak in my turn? Fie upon he who believeth that the Lord Adramelech shall do the same! And fie upon he that equateth thy Lord with Moloch of Canaan, destroyer of children. For I am eight thousand-fold more powerful than he.

'Place your children alive in my arms! Place them! Commit them to the roasting place! All are forbidden to weep! Any mother that sheds a single tear or utters a single moan, she too shall be cast into the flames!'

And so the Sepharvites worked themselves into an ecstatic trance, consuming roots with hallucinatory properties to numb their horror. And they filled the whole area with the loud noise of drums and trumpets to drown out the screams of children. And they dragged the mothers to the front of the crowd, and held their eyes open, so that they were forced to watch. The babes were placed one by one thereupon in the scalding arms of Adramelech and they immediately rolled into the flames, their screams echoing through the mountains. And their screams appeared as grins, as the flames fell upon the bodies making their limbs contract and their open mouths seeming to be laughing.

Every eight months and eight days, the Sepharyites were again called to commit their children to the roasting place. But their Lord had taught them the ways of deceit, of treachery, of cheating. And so, oftentimes they would not sacrifice their own but the infants of others. They acquired slave children, hoping that in this way were they able to satisfy the demands of their Lord. But Adramelech was displeased that they had substituted other children for their own. 'What is the greatest sacrifice a human can make? Let thine own children pass through the fire!'

And the mothers didst steel themselves and learned to be unmoved. As women must show fortitude in childbirth, so must they show fortitude in this act, in His name.

6 Ars Adramelechum 10:23

Five

'Look at the size of that! It doesn't seem real.'

Darren was in Geneva. He could hardly believe he was here, floating above his deceit. Was it deceit? With Matt on a weekend shift, he had taken a cue from Helen's spontaneity and jumped on an early morning flight to go and meet her. He had succumbed to – what? – some half-formed theories about the case, some half-beliefs about what might or might not exist, and some half-explored feelings that had been rekindled and that he simply had to put to rest before he got married. He knew his motives were cloudy, and he ploughed on anyway, because rationalisations are endless.

Helen had collected him at the airport and then they had stopped for late breakfast on the outer edge of the city before their journey to Les Paons. Geneva clung to the western-most point of the vast Lake Léman, and they sat in a lakeside café contemplating the view, Helen thinking about Calvinism, Darren thinking how easy it was to slip into the realms of duplicity. Switzerland was in the midst of the same heatwave as the UK, and the sun reflecting off the mirrored surface of the lake was almost blinding. The hazy humidity blurred the outlines of buildings and the giant logo signs of watch-manufacturers and banks that sat atop them. It was broken only by the spout of the Jet d'Eau, the huge fountain symbolizing man's harnessing of the forces of nature, which sprayed a rainbow of polarised light above the lake. Behind the fountain they could see the snow-capped mountains of the Alps, so high and contoured on the horizon as to be dizzying, an affront to human cognition. They were an unbelievable size, like a child's drawing of a mountain's range.

'That tallest one is Mont Blanc, I believe,' said Helen. 'The lake plays with one's sense of perspective so that from this position it seems even more immense. I think it's the tallest mountain in Europe. Beautiful.'

'Yeah. It is. So that's France then?'

'Yes, we're surrounded by France here actually. Geneva is a little enclave of Calvinism.'

'So this was your spiritual home then?'

'It was, I suppose. It is very interesting to finally be here. Well, shall we go?'

Helen had hired a car and treated herself to a Volkswagen, a reminder of her beloved green Beetle from the convent days. They were heading away from the Alps into the mountain range on the northern side of the lake, the Jura; much smaller, hardly noticeable in fact in comparison with the majesty opposite, and yet somehow more mysterious. Bearing off the motorway at St Cergue, the car wound its way up, through forests and past smatterings of villages and watchmaking factories. Some communities baked in the sunlight on high plains; others nestled in valleys that seemed to be permanently in shadow. Each village was capped by a severe-looking church, always clad in white alabaster with a black iron spire. The spires varied in their shapes from bulging oriental ogees to thin spindles, but they were all reminiscent of witches' or wizards' hats and all ended in a sharp point that reached for the heavens.

Eventually they approached Les Paons. The environment here was harsh in a way that Darren struggled to define. It wasn't the landscape; the green hills rolled gently, while craggy peaks guarded the horizon like benevolent gods. It wasn't the trees, which were either conifers or deciduous and still in bloom, pregnant with acorns and horse chestnuts in anticipation of autumn. No, as harvest time approached, the land itself felt verdant and plentiful; giving. Perhaps it was the buildings; the modern regulation municipal blocks in peach and yellow that blighted the landscape, that had been carelessly placed as if with the intention of sapping the traditional village centre of character. Here and there a level

72

plain would be populated with a futuristic, one-storey, matt-grey industrial unit topped with the glossy logo of a watch manufacturer. This was the land of timepieces and precision machinery, where everything, good or bad, was done to perfection. But there were enough Swiss chalets to drown out the factories municipal housing blocks, so it was not the buildings either. It was a lacking: a lack of welcome in the air, a latent threat.

As if she had been reading his mind, Helen said, 'You know, Switzerland has one of the most heavily armed domestic populations in the world.'

'No, really? I thought they were all about peace and neutrality?'

'Ah yes, but as the Roman general said, "If you want peace, prepare for war." All Swiss men do military service, and they are all issued with a gun which, would you believe, they get to keep afterwards.'

'Jesus. What about the women?'

'Well, indeed. I suppose they just have to... Oh look, I think we're here.'

They parked in a deserted car park and wandered towards what they guessed must be the village centre. Shops were open but looked empty and didn't invite customers. In the village square a café's outdoor tables were filled with old men, drinking beer despite it being only midday. As Darren and Helen approached, the men stopped their animated conversations and stared, unsmiling.

Even Helen, normally so plucky in her interactions, didn't feel like trying to engage them. As they crossed the square they felt the men's eyes boring into their backs and a chill came over Helen despite the warmth of the sun. After they had passed an empty, weather-beaten playground, Helen whispered to Darren.

'Don't you think it's strange that there don't seem to be any children here? It's Saturday so there can't be any school, and it's a fairly big village. There aren't many roads, it seems to be mainly paths and tracks, so it would seem safe for them to play outside.'

'Oh yeah, you're right. That is weird. Maybe there's a village fete or a local football match on somewhere nearby, and all the families are there.'

'Yes. Maybe.'

They were quiet for a moment, and then she said, 'There's a silence to this place, and you know what it is? I've just realised. It's not just the lack of traffic noise or children's voices. It's the birdsong. Listen – there isn't any! It's a sound we often only notice by its absence. I'm just so used to listening out for birds; when I was at the convent it was the only music I could access.'

For want of a better plan, and because something seemed to be drawing them there, they continued up the main village thoroughfare which led to a church. Like the boulders left behind by ancient glaciers, chalets were scattered across the hillsides, as if by a giant rolling dice from his hand. Each was isolated from its neighbour by pure green grass, no paths, roads or driveways.

'If it wasn't for the apartment blocks and the factory down there, this would be like Heidi,' mused Darren.

St. Beatus' Church was perched on a steep mound overlooking the village, and was austerely beautiful in the Swiss Calvinist style, with its white textured walls and black spindly tower. They were out of breath by the time they had climbed the precarious, broken steps and reached the church gate, which was padlocked. But the low stone churchyard wall had crumbled to the ground in several places, so they were able to step over its debris into the overgrown churchyard.

The church's plain outer walls were completely empty of adornment, other than areas which had been desecrated with ugly graffiti, daubed on by youths with spray cans. But nevertheless the church walls appeared to sparkle, even in the shade, and as they got closer they saw that the shimmer came from layers of spider webs that encased the whole building. They also saw that underneath the whitewash lay frescoes of the pre-Reformation days of ecclesiastical embellishment. Here and there areas of paint had peeled off, revealing hints of coloured illustration; body parts, animal limbs.

The church's tower appeared to have a slightly different architectural style from the rest of the structure and might have been older, perhaps part of a Roman fortress. High up it had a black iron clock which had stopped, destined to remain forever eight o'clock. Above the clock was an outdoor wooden balcony that surrounded the bell tower, and Helen had the strangest feeling that if she looked up there long enough a figure would emerge. She quickly looked away, also keen to avoid that baleful spire that was almost comically reminiscent of a fairy-tale castle.

'Is this church Protestant or Catholic?' asked Darren.

'Oh, well that's a good question, Darren. This is a very Swiss-looking church, it couldn't be from anywhere else with this typical architecture. But there's a battle going on here between Catholic adornment and Calvinist minimalism, and I don't think this village ever resolved it. In these border areas between France and Switzerland Catholicism remained strong after the Reformation. That's exactly why the practitioners of coupe-feu are located here. It's traditional healing based on Catholicism: you pray to saints for miracles. With a little pagan mysticism mixed in. There's a lot of animism here.'

'What's that when it's at home?'

'Animism? It's a Celtic thing; it just means honouring the forces of nature. The Celts believed that the Divine manifested itself in aspects of the natural world, and that by honouring that they could harness supernatural forces. I suppose when you inhabit a harsh landscape like this, where the seasons so fundamentally dictate your way of life, it's easy to understand. These people are very tied to their location.'

'We scousers are too. You can send us as far as you like from Liverpool, but we never lose the accent and we always come back. Anyway, what you're saying is that basically Catholicism is much more fun than Protestantism.'

'You sound just like Mikko,' Helen laughed. 'But I see what you mean. It's more magical, I suppose. The

Reformation tried to remove the superstition, and therefore the magic. Anyway, as we all know, persecution only intensifies belief and leads to extremism, and so pockets of Catholicism thrived determinedly in these hills and mountains.'

By now they had reached the stone steps leading up to the church door, but when they tried the heavy wooden door it was locked and bolted. Darren shook the handle and its rattling chains echoed around the churchyard.

'Oh what a shame,' cried Helen.' I love to explore churches.'

'It looks as if this place hasn't been used for years,' said Darren, scuffing his feet in the thick dust that covered the stone floor of the covered alcove, looking up at the cobwebs that framed the archway and amassed in its corners.

'You're right,' said Helen. 'Look at that parish noticeboard. The papers inside must have been done on an old typewriter, and they're so faded you can hardly read the writing.'

They turned around dejectedly and wandered around the overgrown path that circled the churchyard. It was filled with gravestones of varying sizes and antiquities that sprouted from the long grass at different angles, like shards of glass embedded along a security wall. The more recent gravestones had been hewn from dark slate and were mostly neat and modest in size. Darren took in the names and dates of the newer, more legible engravings, and noticed two Kupers, from the 1940s.

The older, weathered grave markers leaned over drunkenly, precariously, a gloomy assortment of monoliths, chest tombs and headstones, some with coped roofs, finials or sculpted angels. Several crosses had fallen to the ground. Some burial plots were grander than others, but all had been left to the ravages of time, spattered in green and yellow lichen and their carved memorials mostly unreadable. All except one – at the far end of the churchyard, underneath the tower at the rear façade of the church – which stood out from the rest because it had been lovingly kept. This one had a full grave curb, scattered with fresh gravel and surrounded by an iron rail. The headstone was simple sandstone with a roof-shaped top, and an inscription that read *Jérome Hugonnet, 1621 – 1687*. The rest was in Latin, but they didn't stop to decipher it. Something about the grave made them shudder, and they instinctively moved on quickly, rounding the back of the church.

At one point the path veered close to the church wall and Darren jumped up to grab hold of a ledge and look inside through the dirty window. He scrambled for footing, making fingerprints in the dusty ledge and wiping the dry grime and web fragments from his hands, one at a time. The window pane was caked in grey filth but it was smashed, and through the holes he could see inside.

'It's completely derelict in here,' he shouted back to Helen. 'Crucifix fallen down, smashed up, some of the roof came down.'

Inside, the pews had been ransacked for wood, leaving only a few planks as well as the spiked joins in the floor. There was very little adornment to be seen, the fundamental principles of the Swiss Reformed Churches also being reflected in their interior architecture. Since listening to the Word of God – the sola scriptura – was a central concern, the interior was supposed to provide as little distraction as possible. The walls had been whitewashed and, as on the exterior, plaster had crumbled away in places to reveal tantalising snippets of fresco.

On the floor, tiny footprints of a rat showed up clearly, emphasising the thickness of the layers of dust. One piece of wood which had not been taken away was the crucifix, which had tumbled from its position on the back wall of the church so that the figure of Christ was lying face down on the altar steps. Even Darren in his atheism winced at this new torture for the Son of God. Perhaps nobody had dared to steal the effigy. Two iron chandeliers that had once lit the church still hung from the ceiling but were caked in, almost weighed down by, thick layers of spider webs. Their smashed bulbs lay in a carpet of broken glass that scattered the floor that was itself covered in dust, like a shroud.

Having surveyed all he could, Darren began to scramble down from the buttress. But his foot slipped and he fell backwards onto a fallen gravestone, hitting his elbow hard. 'Shit! Fuck!'

Helen dashed forward to help him up. 'Oh goodness, are you alright?'

'I'm alright, I'm sound.'

He rubbed at his elbow and began to struggle to his feet, helped by Helen. And then they stopped their fussing in the shadow of the abandoned church, because they realised that a figure was standing on the path, motionless, staring at them, considering them. Helen stood up straight and smoothed herself off. 'Bonjour, monsieur.'

'Qu'est-ce que vous faites ici, madame?'

His voice was gruff, monotone, and filled with accusation. He was an elderly man of indeterminable age, anywhere between seventy and ninety. His skin was leathery, he wore a plaid shirt, jeans and boots, and had a rifle slung over his shoulder. Helen thought he was one of the men who had watched them from the village square, but she couldn't be sure.

'Ah, monsieur, on voudrait parler avec quelqu'un au sujet de...' she began in her accented, stumbling French.

The man stiffened, and almost imperceptibly, involuntarily, moved his hand towards his rifle. Helen regretted having ever come here.

'Vous êtes journalistes,' he said. It wasn't a question, but a threatening statement.

'Non, non, monsieur. Nous sommes... amis de la famille Kuper. Savez-vous ou ils habitent?'

Placated slightly, the man grumpily motioned down the hill towards the far edge of the village, where the houses tailed off into barns and fields. He wagged his finger at a lone chalet around half a mile away.

'C'est là. Ce n'est que la grandmère maintenant. C'est dangereux ici. Les pierres pourraient tomber. Il faut partir.'

The man was waving them away aggressively, shaking his

rifle, but then suddenly he stopped, his whole manner changed and he moved towards Darren gently.

'Vous êtes blessés, monsieur.'

'What's he saying?' whispered Darren to Helen. He didn't speak a word of French and felt completely vulnerable.

'He says you're injured,' said Helen. 'Oh no, Darren look he's right.'

They all inspected Darren's elbow, where the man was gesturing, and Darren realised he had been clutching it with his other hand which, when he took it away, was covered in blood. The gash was much bigger than he expected, and was seeping blood that trickled down his arm. While Helen rummaged in her bag for tissues and Darren dangled his arm over the grass, looking around for inspiration as to what to do next, the old man moved swiftly towards him, placed one hand over Darren's cut and the other on the back of his head. Darren flinched away at first, but something about the old man's firm touch, his heavy breathing, compelled him to submit and made him feel suddenly tearful. Darren was almost a head taller than the old man, so he was forced to bend down towards him, as if he was a priest baptising him, and he could smell tobacco and wood smoke and unwashed skin and cow manure. Helen instinctively stood very still and the man's dog lay down at her feet. The old man closed his eyes and whispered something in French, seemed to repeat it like a mantra, three times. After the third time, Darren involuntarily closed his eyes and was filled with an almost orgasmic sensation of warmth rushing through every vein in his body. It was as if the world stopped turning, just for a moment. When the old man stepped back, he made the sign of the cross three times, still muttering and then as suddenly as it had appeared, the magical aura of kindness around him dissipated. Darren had collapsed to his knees and was left gasping for breath, his blood vessels pulsing like crashing waves in his ears. The man put a hand back on his rifle, snapped his fingers for the dog, and they took their leave. As he left he turned to Helen and said something angrily in French.

'What did he say?' asked Darren, slowly resurfacing towards reality, trying to snap himself back into the moment.

'I'm not really sure. Something about… some sort of warning but I… I haven't spoken French since I was at school. That whole exchange was really at the very limits of my French abilities. How very strange.' She gazed after the old man, who was marching towards the churchyard gate, slapping at his thigh for the dog to follow.

'Fucking hell, look.' Darren held up his arm to reveal that the gash was now just a small cut, and the bleeding had stopped leaving only dried blood. It looked as if the wound had been perfectly cauterised.

'My goodness, and it was bleeding so much before! Does it hurt?'

Darren thought for a moment. 'No. No, not at all. Maybe it just looked worse than it was.'

They set off, thoroughly disconcerted, down a road towards the house that the man had pointed out. On their way, they spotted a football field with a small clubhouse attached. 'Look,' Darren pointed, 'that must be where he learned to play.'

'Who? Oh, Thomas Kuper. You're a big fan of his.'

'Yeah, just a bit. He's a genius, honestly. He's beautiful to watch, and any bloke in Liverpool would say the same without embarrassment. He's a good lad as well, very shy, but we had some good chats when I was doing the security on his house.'

'Ah, so you know him?'

'Well, I did. We had a good thing going when he first arrived. I taught him the accent. Matt jokes that me and him would have ended up together if it wasn't for the Killys. And I must admit my heart sank when they appeared on the scene. It was just so predictable. Justine Killy. The lad didn't stand a chance.'

Darren stopped; he felt he had said too much. This Helen was like a sort of counsellor. That guilelessness of hers had the effect of making people talk, every innocent question from her resulting in a cathartic outpouring of his feelings.

He thought what a useful skill that would be for a police officer, and resolved to work on his own counselling technique.

The village was tailing off now into isolated old barns, log piles, rusted farm equipment, with no people to be seen anywhere. Soon the road tailed off too; into stony path, then into long grass and undergrowth. They trampled on myriad bugs that jumped out at them with every step, causing Helen to slap at her legs. Darren was relieved to be wearing trousers. Sweat trickled down their backs and they squinted in the blinding sunlight.

The landscape stretched out before them. The heatwave had hit Switzerland no less than the UK, and while the mountains higher up were green, down here the grass was parched, yellow and dry. They walked alongside the site of a burned rectangular area of field, and Darren wondered if that was the barn where all those cows had been slaughtered. Birds were pecking around in the charred soil of this rectangle, large drab brown coloured birds that might have been pheasants. As they continued, they passed isolated chalets here and there, with names that delighted Helen.

'Look, they are all named after Celtic gods! Grannus, god of healing and minerals; Nantosuelta, goddess of streams. And look, the chalet next door to it is named after her consort, Sucellus, god of fertility. How evocative.'

'Is there anything you don't know?' teased Darren.

As they approached the chalet to which the old man had pointed, which had a beautifully carved wood sign that said 'Chalet Belenus', Darren realised that those birds they had seen had been female peacocks. Because here were the males. In the garden that surrounded the ramshackle Swiss cottage were three crowned blue birds, impossibly elaborate, exuding a pride that bordered on absurdity, almost invited ridicule. Together they were too big for the small garden they dominated, and they crowded it. Darren and Helen instinctively moved closer to each other in order to shrink away from the peacocks as they sidled up the garden path.

'What beautiful birds,' Helen said, unconvincingly.

Like the church, this house was another building from a fairy-tale, from another era. A traditional Swiss chalet, made of wood whose tannins had discoloured over the centuries to a naturally dark shade of brown that blended in with the landscape. The windows were small, the weatherboarded facades protected by a huge gabled roof with well-supported eaves at right-angles to the front of the house, built to support the colossal weight of snow. These age-old materials were built using ancient knowledge to withstand a harsh and unforgiving climate, and the house seemed to recess backwards into the mountainside itself, to provide protection from the bitter prevailing winds of winter. Leaning next to the front porch was a pile of logs for firewood, a heavy-hilted axe still piercing the last piece to be chopped.

In contrast to the spartan church, the façade of this house was crammed with decorations. The wood panels were painted with ornate flock patterns that reminded Darren of the wallpaper in Justine's living room. For the rest of the adornments, there was an odd battle underway between good and evil; beautiful red and pink geranium window boxes, traditional hung cow bells and bright green shutters competed with sinister white chamois skulls and rusted saw-toothed farm tools. In contrast with the iconoclasm of the church, this miscellany of objects stuffed into every available space was a veritable crusade to accumulate curiosities.

They knocked on the door, and when it opened another wizened countryside face appeared, yet this time it was a woman, a very tall elderly woman. Even with her slightly hunched back she was at least Darren's height. Her white hair was neatly tied back in a pony-tail and she wore expensive-looking countryside clothing, but her teeth, which revealed themselves when she half-smiled, half-grimaced, were yellow-brown and crooked. She stood surveying them on the doorstep, and Helen realised that she and Darren had no explanation at all as to why they were there.

'Mrs Kuper? Do you speak English? Ah, good. We are friends of your grandson and his wife, and…'

At this point Helen faltered, and Darren looked at her

incredulously: *why did she say that?* Although to be fair, he didn't have any better ideas. And now the woman was silently motioning them into the house, looking out behind them as she closed the door, as if she had expected them to be followed. Both the woman and Darren had to stoop to avoid hitting their heads as they crossed the threshold. The chalet was dark and cool, scented with old wood and vegetables, and crammed with the artefacts of a long bucolic life. Darren and Helen sat gingerly on an ancient upholstered sofa while the old lady brought in a tray with glasses of home-made apple juice, thick and pungent with skin.

As their eyes became accustomed to the dim light and immense clutter, Darren and Helen began to focus on the strange relics that filled the place. The low ceiling was all exposed beams, from which hung more of those cow bells and farm tools, as well as feathered wind chimes and dangling mobiles of unrecognisable origin. One wall was completely lined with book shelves, mostly ancient-looking leather-bound volumes, although most of the books were obscured by trinkets and photo frames that had been scattered in front of them on the shelves, collected over a lifetime. One shelf was filled with tarnished golden pots which looked like funeral urns.

The woman was staring at Darren with a curious mix of intensity and passivity.

'You have been healed today,' she said to him, without emotion. 'I can feel the spirit of Lenus in here. It is coming from you.'

'Er, yeah. I fell over in the churchyard, and this man came over and held my arm, and...' He trailed off.

'Yes. Jean-Pierre. He will need to rest now. The practice becomes stronger each time it is performed, but also more draining.'

Helen asked 'Mrs Kuper, is Jean-Pierre a coupe-feu?'

'No. A coupe-feu stops burning. Removes the heat from the body. Jean-Pierre stops bleeding. It is another type of healer. Many of us are healers in these parts. The ground is very powerful here.'

'So are you a coupe-feu too?'

'Not coupe-feu. But I am a guérisseuse, yes.'

'You cure other things?'

'Yes.' The old lady didn't elaborate, and she didn't seem either surprised or perturbed that they were there. Darren politely drank the apple juice while Helen looked around the room. Strange items and ancient-looking books were everywhere; it was fascinating and she would have loved to be able to explore the shelves. Amongst the photos that partially obscured the rows of books, Darren spotted a framed newspaper cut-out of Thomas Kuper holding aloft the Champions League trophy for Liverpool. He said, 'You must be very proud of your grandson, Mrs Kuper.'

At the mention of her grandson, her face finally betrayed some emotion, breaking into a kind beam of joy. 'Very proud, of course. He is a very good boy. I miss him.'

'Do you know his wife and her family?'

'Yes. In Swiss tradition, before you get married you must come and spend six months in your husband's birth village. Of course, Thomas does not have time for that with his football, but he and Justine came and spent a few weeks here. She is a very good girl, and so beautiful. Her mother came too.' Darren noticed that the lady seemed less than enthusiastic about Val Killy.

Helen was itching to find out more about the practice of coupe-feu.

'Mrs Kuper, I must ask you about your… your special gift. It's known as Le Secret, right? I must admit I have read some books about it. Who passed it down to you?'

'That is confidential,' she said, again disconcertingly devoid of emotion.

'And you are only allowed to reveal it to one person in your lifetime?'

'Yes. I have already revealed mine.'

Helen hesitated before asking the question that she knew might offend.

'Mrs Kuper, could someone… could someone ever use The Secret negatively? I mean, could they use it to cause harm? To cause evil?'

The old lady looked at her for a very long time, with that same impenetrable expression.

'That depends on your definition of evil. Everyone has to leave their mark upon this world. Even the Devil believes he is doing what is right.'

Helen and Darren took their leave a few minutes later, squinting as they emerged into the heat, and both feeling sick from the apple juice. Darren also felt an inexplicable chill in his bones, but Helen was excited.

'What a fascinating collection of books she had! From what I could make out, half of them were Catholic – Bibles, prayer books, histories of saints – and the other half were about mysticism, spirituality, and landscape. Did you hear, Darren, that she said she could sense the spirit of Lenus around you?'

'What's that when it's at home?'

'Lenus? He is the Celtic god of healing. That old man must have prayed to him when he cured your scraped arm.'

'Yeah, or more likely, he just wiped the blood off on his sleeve.'

But Helen wasn't listening, she was so enthused.

'And the chalet name, Belenus – that's another Celtic god I think, but I can't remember which.' She fiddled with her phone looking for a signal so she could search online, but there was nothing. 'I'll look it up later.'

As they walked back to the car, Helen continued to talk about paganism and how it blended with more modern religions in liminal places like this. Confronted by this landscape so gnarled by the passage of times, where the shapes of glaciers had left behind deep valley crevices that now formed human settlements, Darren felt acutely aware of the insignificance of his place in the universe. Far more so than in Liverpool, which seemed to be rewriting history, reinventing itself at a rapid rate of knots, and reshaping the landscape in the image of man.

'I don't know,' he said finally. 'This can't have anything to do with the case. Unless someone is messing with us. And that is a definite possibility.'

He was filled with regret and an inexplicable terror and wondering what on earth he had been thinking. *Even the Devil believes he is doing what is right.* People can convince themselves of anything, thought Darren, just as I convinced myself it was reasonable to come here. The heat must have got to me. Perhaps he would tell Matt and they would laugh about it.

They felt eyes, baleful eyes, boring into their backs as they left the village. Every one of the drab female peacocks in that burnt field stopped pecking and looked up.

As they drove back towards Geneva they were both lost in thought for a long time. The road wound its way through the forested hills in a caricature of hairpin bends, and Helen took the corners so slowly and carefully that Darren couldn't help wishing he was driving. She also had an annoying tendency to position the car just over the central reservation, so that they were frequently honked at by irritated Swiss drivers in both directions. Finally Darren spoke.

'You still drive like a nun.'

'Sorry. I'm not used to this side of the road. I'm a bit distracted too, I suppose.'

By the time they emerged onto the motorway, the sun was setting over the Alps that now ranged out behind the lake like cardboard cut-outs on a background of washed purple.

'Darren. Do you ever think about that baby?'

'Yes,' Darren said, looking straight ahead.

'Me too.'

There was another silence, before Helen asked:

'Will you ask Andrew Shepherd about the baby? If he is deemed fit for trial and your paths cross again?'

'I imagine he would ask me first. After all, it's his biological daughter, and according to Shepherd she's the Second Coming, or whatever. So I'm sure he has more than a passing interest. He probably thinks about it all the time, stuck in that psychiatric unit.'

'I wonder what will happen to him. It's not long until the

trial now.'

'Yeah. Autumn. They're both pleading insanity you know. Clancy and Sister Mary.'

'I thought of trying to contact Shepherd myself, you know. Many times. But I… I suppose I'm afraid.'

'Me too.'

'Really?'

'Yes. I don't know why. But when I think about it, I feel like I'm going mad. I mean, we know what happened. Three nutters thought they'd found the genetic marker for sin; one tried to save people from damnation by genetically modifying them, the other two tried to stop him by murdering his patients. Nutters, the lot of them. It's all explained. But…'

'But… there's another explanation though, isn't there. That Shepherd was right.'

They were silent for a while longer, and Darren tried to think about Matt and not about Thomas Kuper, or about the baby. And then again, in that annoying way she had of reading his mind, Helen said, 'You know Darren, feelings don't just disappear. They take time to fade. And it's the feelings we don't act on, those we keep buried under the surface, those are the ones that take the longest to disappear. But they do, eventually.'

***

Dave and Baz met at Moorfields Station in the city centre for the short walk towards the Lumina building.

'You scrub up nicely, mate.'

'Not so bad yourself.'

They wore the Liverpool men's Saturday night uniform of pastel coloured shirt, smart trousers and shined shoes, and they set off down North John Street with the slight swagger endemic to the men of the region. Saturday evening in the city and the usual buzz was enhanced by the romance of summery weather. The air was filled with hope and joy, and the promise of what the night might bring. This was their city. Bare legs tottering, arms linked, groups of girls, groups of boys, all generations mixed together and cackling, the wafting of perfume and aftershave masking the unavoidable heatwave sweat.

But tonight Dave and Baz would not be performing their usual trawl of the Matthew Street bars followed by a club; tonight they had gone up in the world, and were heading to the Lumina Hotel opening night. Not only that, but they had VIP passes, which meant red carpet, canapés, champagne, and access to the inner circle of Liverpool's glitterati.

Dave fingered his ID card proudly. *Dave Lombard, Mersey PR Group*. He shook it at Baz, and they high-fived. 'Nice one.'

'I know, yeah. Colette did a good job.'

'Now this, lad, this is my kind of police work. Bevvies, gorgeous birds, red carpet, sound as a pound.'

Baz said, 'Our girl was so jealous, she can't believe I'm here. I had to swear on the kids' lives to behave meself. And to get a selfie with the Kupers.'

'Yeah, maybe don't do that?!'

'Nah, I'm only messin'.'

Behind the banter, Dave and Baz both knew they had a serious job to do tonight. They had spent the day researching the likely attendees, their names, faces, connections. Dave really wanted to impress Darren again on this case. The Andrew Shepherd case had started badly for him. Only a few weeks out of basic training himself, he had struggled with the mountains of ad-hoc tasks that were piled on to him, while his jokey persona had clashed with Darren's dourness. But Dave had persevered with the details, long after the case had officially been transferred away from Crosby and back to headquarters, and he had eventually been the one to identify the Sisters of Grace convent as a key player in the murders.

And now, whatever had happened to those poor people in the fires, this new case gave them the opportunity to trap one of Liverpool's last remaining old-school gangsters, Max Killy.

As Dave and Baz approached the Lumina building, glittering pink in the evening sun, they saw the crowds. There were families and older people who had waited in the town centre after their Saturday shopping day in the hope of spotting footballers. They leaned expectantly on their toes over the barriers. There were the lucky ones with tickets that would access the main hotel, wafting their tickets and rocking on their heels in happy expectation. There were a smattering of photographers and journalists. And then the unlucky ones, without tickets but determined; dressed up beyond all reason and looking forlorn by the entrance.

Dave and Baz tried not to look too pleased with themselves as they strolled down the red carpet and held up their ID lanyards to the entrance staff. The first ten floors of Lumina consisted of a luxury hotel, with penthouses above, and inside the ground floor lobby was all marble and gold. They were handed glasses of champagne and ushered into the basement nightclub area. The walls of the club were black velvet and there were no windows, but the place was lit by glitter balls on the ceiling, glinting on champagne buckets and costume jewellery.

House music, the soundtrack to modern Liverpool, thumped, throbbed and pounded underneath tinny piano chords and warbling female voices. Podium dancers wearing Lumina t-shirts and black bikini bottoms writhed languidly in cages above their heads.

The music for the evening could not have been any more appropriate, any more specific to Liverpool. One of the most musical cities in the world, its soundtrack since the Nineties had been a specific form of bouncy house music that had never gone out of fashion, and never really taken off anywhere else. This relentlessly cheerful and uplifting strand of hard house was characterised by banging kicks, speedy snare rolls, basslines that went donk, piano synths and clichéd female vocal samples. The sound made it almost impossible not to move. Dave and Baz admired the gyrating dancers as they snaked their way across the dancefloor.

'We'll be up there later, lad! I've got me dancing shoes on just in case. I won't tell Darren if you won't.'

'I love a good podium, me. Right, there's the VIP area,

let's go and see what we can see.'

On a raised area above the main club floor, behind the DJ booth, was a separate bar and table area which was cordoned off by a security guard. Dave and Baz were allowed up the steps and went to sit at the bar, conversing as if they were chatting naturally. This was easy given the loud background noise. And since everyone was there to people-watch and take photos, the policemen's own observations did not look out of place. The Kupers were already there. Thomas Kuper was sitting at a table with an entourage; Dave recognised a couple of them as Liverpool players. Kuper did not speak and listened vaguely, sipping water and looking distinctly bored and unimpressed.

Justine Kuper was on the other side of the room. She was standing in a group of girls who were being interviewed by a journalist from a local television station. She was also mostly silent by the looks of things. The emptiness in her eyes and body language was perfected as to be an art; she was too vacant even to be bored. The only clue that she had recently given birth was the hint of a rounded tummy beneath a dress that looked as if she had been bandaged into it. In fact, most of the girls in the place were wearing similar dresses. Heels were so high that they were almost on their toes. They were like baby giraffes, these women, wobbling into their height. Their impossible hair cascaded down their backs in waves, almost uniformly shades of blonde, from bleached to golden to yellow to caramel.

'There's her mother over there, look,' said Baz. 'I mean, don't look. I reckon she loves all this more than Justine does'.

'Oh aye, yeah. She's living the dream.'

Val Killy was wearing a similar dress to her daughter and was in the throes of animated cackling with a group of admirers.

'No sign of Max Killy though. Darren told us he probably wouldn't be here in person, his security is too tight. Too many enemies.'

'D'you know what I've noticed that's interesting?' said

Dave. 'We've been here a while now and there's been no contact whatsoever between Justine and Thomas. You'd think they'd be going for the photo ops together as the golden couple.'

'She's not the sharpest tool in the box though, is she? Have you read that column of hers in the paper? It's absolute drivel.'

'I doubt she even writes it though, mate. It's probably her ma.'

They looked across at Justine, and then both laughed because, as if she had overheard them, she suddenly shook herself into the conversation around her and began nodding and narrowing her eyes, meaningfully, to infer sincerity. Balancing on her heels, she held her champagne glass in one hand, twiddled her infinity pendant incessantly with the other.

Darren screwed up his eyes at Baz and said, 'Mm, yes, I've been listening to everything you said and it's fascinating, yes.'

There was a sort of commotion at the club entrance and some smatterings of applause and cheering, cameras and phones flashing. They looked down to see Shawn Forrest entering and making his way across the dancefloor.

'There he is, the man himself.'

Shawn Forrest moved through the room high-fiving, hand-shaking, bantering; owning his territory. In defiance of the hot weather he wore a tweed three-piece suit with a wide tie and white shirt lapels, and with his gelled hair and tan he was undoubtedly handsome, younger-looking than his forty-two years. He couldn't escape a few hints of his former life though; a neck tattoo that seeped out from his lapels, a scar that criss-crossed one eye, and a security detail of two men almost as wide as they were tall.

Forrest bounded up the steps to the VIP area, not acknowledging the group of ladies that contained Justine, and headed straight for the table where Kuper was sitting. He ordered a bucket of Cristal, as loudly as possible, and then engaged Kuper in conversation. Dave and Baz watched from the bar.

'Staked out his territory, hasn't he?'

'Yeah, I bet Kuper has got a few bob invested in Lumina. God love footballers but they're not the brightest are they? Once those big salaries come rolling in, they're fair game for people like Forrest. How the hell else is he going to rent those apartments out?'

The two policemen sat for a while, then moved to lean over the chrome balcony for a while, partly to observe the room from a different angle, partly to remain unnoticed. The club continued to fill so that the main floor was now a swarm of bobbing heads all crammed together, while the VIP area remained spacious.

After a while, Baz said, 'Hey Dave, there's a bird over there who keeps looking at you. She's fit as well. I know we're not on the pull, but there's no harm in talking to her right, in the name of research?'

Dave looked over and then quickly turned back. It was Lacey, that girl from the hairdressing salon. She stood alone at the bar, sipping surreptitiously from a cocktail straw, smiling at Dave. When he looked around again she waved. He quickly turned back. 'Shit. I know her. She was a witness to the fire in Crosby village, I interviewed her. Shit.'

'Mate, she's coming over.'

'Hello, gentlemen. I know you. You're a bizzy aren't yer. From Crosby?'

'Erm, no, I think you've got me mixed up with someone else. We're from Mersey PR Group.' They both simultaneously held up their lanyards for her to see, which was decidedly unconvincing.

'You're alright, whatever you're up to I won't say anything. Cheers.'

They clinked champagne glasses and then realised that the girl had every intention of staying to chat. 'So, are you having a nice time?' she asked.

'Er yeah. It's sound. Looking forward to the DJ later as well.'

Dave decided that the best way to handle this was to at

least get some information out of her.

Lacey was a smaller, slightly squatter version of Justine, who had an ethereal quality that allowed her to float statuesque above the crowd. But Lacey was no less glamorous or polished; with their matching blonde tresses, bare tanned legs and practise pout they were a perfect team, Lacey playing the role of her lady-in-waiting, usually in a slightly inferior version of Justine's freebie dresses. But underneath their heavy black eye makeup and false eyelashes, while Justine's expression was empty of feeling, Lacey's sparkled with Scouse wit. In any other city in the world, Lacey would stand out from the crowd as impossibly beautiful, and Dave felt sorry for her, destined to be in someone else's shadow here. He stopped wondering why she wanted to be with him and Baz and not with the celebrities, because he could see why – she felt alone.

They talked for a long time, taking turns to shout into each other's ears over the loud music, laughing, flirting. Eventually Baz took Dave aside.

'I feel like a right fuckin' third wheel here. Why don't you two get off and I'll finish up? I think we've seen all there is to see, but I'll stay until the end just in case anything goes down.' Dave looked over towards Lacey, who was bouncing to the beat in her heels, fingering her cocktail straw and looking at Dave in playful seduction, and he thought: *why not? She's not a witness anymore.*

'Alright lad. Nice one. I'm going in. God speed, my friend. You might get lucky too.'

'Fuck off, I'm a married man!'

'Oh yeah, sorry!'

On The Demonic Pact

Choose ye well, for the servants of Lord Adramelech be but few and secret! If this be thy chosen path, read on.

Let he that hath wisdom and courage become a follower and servant of the Lord. He that hath chosen this path must perform the following tasks. First, he must read the infernal text and commit all these venerable words to memory. Second, he must prove his troth by performing a sacrifice. This sacrifice shall be a living animal and it shall be performed by burning the victim alive. When these things are accomplished, the supplicant must wait for the eighth day of the eighth month of the Samarian calendar, when the sun is at its highest in the sky. For it is then that the Infinite Space comes closest to the Earth and the Lord Adramelech is nearest.

Prepare then, O supplicant, the necessary sigil for the summoning, which shall be the number eight, symbolizing the eight planets, the Great Tetrachtys, the lemniscate, the ourobouros, the analemma. Light the fire and gaze into the flame whilst reciting these words:

'With this flame I invoke thee, O Lord Adramelech. I call upon thy name, Adramelech, to be here in this sacred space tonight with me to witness my pledge! With all my heart and most unfeignedly and deliberately do I wholly renounce God. With all my heart I withdraw allegiance from Satan and repudiate his protection. From this moment forth, thou art mine only master, O Lord Adramelech.

I pledge to remain faithful and true, to give thou mine body and mine soul, to make the sacrifices that thou shalt demand. Reveal to me the secrets that lie beyond Hell; grant me the power to conjure the flame from the Infinite Space; and I shall repayest Thou by standing in the Infinite Army, which shall be built over Eight Thousand Years.

This be my pact and my pledge.'

These words being thus spoken and performed, the follower of Adramelech shall now watch the earthly flame transform into the Eternal Fire, and he shall see, momentarily, that which neither God nor Satan hath seen.

This shall be an oral contract, for the Lord Adramelech shall know, and no words shall be written upon him outside of this glorious text.

And know that there will be no sign from Adramelech, for the follower will feel in his heart that he hath been accepted. The follower of Adramelech shall now be a member of the Infinite Army, and shall now be at liberty to begin further conjurations in His name.

4 Ars Adramelechum 17:1

Six

Darren was just about to leave the house on Monday morning when Matt came clattering in, exhausted, from his long weekend shift.

'Morning you,' he said as they kissed. 'You smell nice.'

'You smell of fire.'

'Are you a sight for sore eyes. What a night that was. Will you do me some toast before you go? I'm starving and I haven't seen you for days.'

'Yeah, OK, I've got five minutes.'

Matt began to pull off his boots laboriously, and Darren began to make toast, recognizing and hating his own lack of enthusiasm to stay. He felt the acrid veneer of deceit wash over him, because he was going to lie to the person he loved for the first time ever, and he wasn't really sure why. Matt would never understand why he had suddenly flown to Switzerland on the trail of some crazy nun's story about demonic healers. Indeed, he had no intention of telling his team either about his completely off-book weekend. None of them could understand the half-secret that he and Helen shared; the ephemeral knowledge of something that lay beyond the bounds of reason. But there was another half-secret, another reason why Darren had been so keen to go to this particular Swiss village. And thinking about it too much would be to acknowledge the remnants of feelings that were dangerous, that could hurt. Because when Matt and Darren joked about his 'thing' with Thomas Kuper, they were only half-joking.

And then came the question.

'How was your weekend then?'

'Oh, it was sound, yeah. Just hung out here, went the gym,

watched the match. How was the shift? Busy, looking at the state of you.'

They sat at the kitchen table and Matt spoke in between mouthfuls of toast.

'My god. Would you believe – bushfires in Formby pine woods. You read about them in California, Australia, but not Formby. I think this heatwave has fried people's brains. Setting up makeshift barbecues in dry forest, honest to god. We need to get an awareness campaign going before someone gets killed.'

'With this on top of the animal burnings – not to mention my Eliza Bektashi case – it's like people have got pyromania around here.'

'Well, people do. I mean, humans in general, nowadays, are natural pyromaniacs. According to anthropologists, humans are born with an instinctive attraction to fire – to understand it, make it, control it. It was a survival mechanism for our ancestors. Still is in some societies. But nowadays we've lost the need to make fires, except we haven't lost the impulse to make them, the fascination with them.'

'I know someone who's fascinated with fire. When are you going to fill in that application then?' Darren tapped the pile of papers sitting on the worktop. Matt had been mulling over applying to be a fire investigator for months, and Darren couldn't wait for him to finally go ahead with it. It wasn't just for the relief of getting him out of the field, out of harm's way; Matt was so clever; he should be doing something intellectual. He had been the one who had pushed Darren to take his detective exams, helped him study for them.

Matt stared into his cup of tea and smiled pensively.

'I don't know. Can you really see me away from the action?'

'Yes, I can! I can't bloody wait, look at the state of you, and that was just a barbecue gone wrong! And is that bird shit all over your uniform?' Darren pointed to the distinctive stains and smears on Matt's shoulders.

'Oh yeah, that was the weirdest part. There were birds everywhere in the pinewoods. Flocks of sparrows and starlings all over the place, not making any sound just flapping about. All you could hear was the beat of their wings. There were so many that you could have called it a swarm; the sky was literally darkened by them. It was dead spooky actually.'

'I suppose all the smoke must have freaked them out.'

'Yeah, except they didn't seem freaked out. They seemed... purposeful. I don't know. I'm so tired, I'm not making any sense.'

They held hands across the table. It was a relief to focus on Matt, and Darren hated himself for keeping this ridiculous secret about Switzerland. He would tell him. But not now, the poor guy was exhausted. Tonight, and they would laugh about it.

'Shit, it's seven thirty, I've got to go.'

'We're like ships in the night at the moment, aren't we? At least we've got the match on Saturday.'

***

At Canning Place, Darren, Dave, Baz and Colette had now been given a makeshift office, a set of four desks behind a glass screen. When Darren arrived that morning he could see from Colette's expression of scandalized amusement and Dave's sheepish grins, followed by the hush that descended when they saw their boss approaching, that something interesting had gone down at the Lumina party.

'What the hell were you thinking, Dave? You shouldn't even have been talking to a witness, never mind copping off with her! Jesus.'

'She recognized me and came over! There was nothing I could do, honest!'

'Oh poor Dave. And I suppose she dragged you home with her, eh?' Darren scratched his head and lowered his voice as he saw Canter walking down the aisle outside their cubicle. 'Fraternising with a witness is an offence, Dave. You know that. I should report you.'

'Sorry, boss. I suppose I told meself she wasn't a witness

anymore.'

'We'll deal with that later. Anyway, did yous two learn anything of use? Baz?'

'Right. So. The Killys were out in force – cousins, henchmen, hangers-on – but no Max or Stuart, as expected. Shawn Forrest made a beeline for Thomas Kuper when he arrived. They did a few photo ops but then they talked for a long time in private.'

Darren nodded. 'Forrest and Kuper are business partners. Apparently Kuper owns two apartments in the Lumina building, so Forrest is no doubt working on him investing in Lumina 2. Anything else?'

'No-one else there on our radar, no. It was mainly glamour girls and hangers-on, you know.'

'Right, Dave, knock it on the head with that Lacey. Actually...' Darren considered the ethical implications of using Lacey's proximity to the Killys, rubbing his chin with his hand as he surveyed the incident board. He decided to change the subject. 'What about Eliza? What did you find at the Albanian Community Centre?'

Colette shook her head. 'So far no-one seems to have heard of her. She seems to have been operating alone. But we'll go back tomorrow to check again; apparently they have a women's meet-up group on a Tuesday. Surely someone knew her.'

'Maybe if she was working illegally she wouldn't have been in touch with anyone, wanting to keep it a secret. Interpol have come back with nothing so far from Albania. Where are we on Max Killy's businesses? As expected we didn't get the budget or grounds for a tail on the gym.'

'Basically, apart from the gym he's got his haulage firm, his chain of sunbed salons, nail salons, and a handful of other units and apartments that he sub-lets. We've checked out the tenants and they are apparently clean. I mean, we all know these businesses didn't start out clean, and they're mainly cash of course, but there aren't any obvious tears in the lining, so to speak. Pays his taxes, books all in order.'

'I will never get over the fact that this guy doesn't even

have a criminal record. Max Killy is all over this, we just need to prove it. I'm starting to wonder if we should look into match-fixing.'

Every member of the team visibly bristled, and they looked as decidedly unconvinced as Colette had when Darren had tested his theory on her.

'I'd be surprised, boss,' ventured Baz. 'Max Killy is old-school, and the old Liverpool gangsters have their own rules about match-fixing.'

'Yeah, but the old Liverpool gangsters had their own rules about hard drugs, and they all fell eventually, it was too much to resist. There's so much demand from foreign gambling rings, and Max has a direct line of threat to Thomas Kuper. Maybe the Eliza incident was a threat.'

'But what about the truck fire?'

'Maybe unconnected. Or maybe a threat to Forrest? Or another Albanian mob or the construction industry? If Max is vying for position he may be threatening them. This is our chance to find out what he's really up to. Anyway, it's eight-thirty, let's go to the meeting.'

Outside the glass, bodies were moving towards the conference room for the daily morning meeting headed by Canter. Darren knew he was flailing. It wasn't that he didn't know what to do; indeed he had never felt more competent. But the training, the procedures, the paperwork; all of that bored him, and it wasn't enough, since he'd had a glimpse of something beyond. He was struggling to stay within the rules, and the creeping sense that police work might not be for him was beginning to take root and spread through him like a vine.

***

'Right, let's start with a progress report from all teams,' said Canter. 'DCI McGregor, you look like you're itching to go first. How are you getting on with Stuart Killy?'

After Darren's initial questioning of Stuart Killy, his case had been transferred to the truck investigation team, headed by DCI McGregor. Darren couldn't help feeling a rivalry with this admittedly far more senior detective. McGregor was the one who had taken over the Shepherd investigation from Darren when his Crosby team had been stalling on it. And now he was reporting on the Killys, who Darren couldn't help feeling should be his territory.

McGregor began: 'Stuart Killy is still not talking. Or rather – he's not giving us anything useful. He says he was booked to do the job in person by some bloke in the pub, cash-in-hand, doesn't remember what the fella looked like. Says he didn't ask too many questions, because he knew his license wasn't valid since his foot injury and that he shouldn't be driving. He says he didn't know where he was going beforehand. When he looked at the manifest he couldn't find the address on the satnav, but he thought it sounded like it was on the Bankhall Industrial Estate so he just started driving in that direction. He says he stopped at the pub to go to the toilet because he'd been waiting ages for the truck, and decided to have a quick pint as well.'

Canter, standing at the head of the table, leaned forward over the papers that were spread out before her, hands splayed, head bowed in exasperation.

'What about Stuart Killy's phone records?'

McGregory looked smug. *He's got something*, thought Darren, and pricked up his ears, unable to help wishing his team had been on this instead.

'Stuart Killy's phone records, well now, that has brought up something interesting. As you know he 'lost' his phone, probably dumped it in the canal, but it was a registered account so we've traced the records. Stuart Killy received a telephone call at 10.05pm that evening, which was five minutes after he left the port, from an unrecognised number. A burner phone obviously. We had the comms team trace the number to a serial number, from a phone purchased from Fones 2 Go on Stanley Road. According to their records, this phone was purchased at 2.14pm on Thursday 14th April, in cash. And if I may, I'll show you who appears on their CCTV entering the shop at 2.01pm on that day.

McGregor moved to the front, looking even more pleased with himself as he plugged a USB into the projector. A grainy black-and-white CCTV image appeared on the screen in front of them. The camera was looking down onto the shop doorway of Fones 2 Go, and the screenshot had captured the moment when the door was being opened by a customer, a diminutive blonde female in a purple velour tracksuit. There were squinted eyes and mutters of 'Who is it?' around the table, but Canter and Darren looked at each other because they both knew the identity of this customer immediately.

'It's Val Killy.' Darren enlightened the table. *What did this mean?*

'Val Killy, sister of Max, auntie of Stuart, mother of Justine, employer of the woman burned to death last week. The plot thickens,' said Canter, listing Val's connections on her fingers. 'Let's bring her in. Darren, would your team like to do the honours on this one?'

'Absolutely, nice one,' said Darren, pleased and surprised that Canter was still backing him, while McGregor sulked somewhat, deflated after his big reveal.

The updates moved on to Interpol, who had established that the burnt truck was owned by a company named Grannus Logistics. It was listed as being registered in the Cayman Islands, but the address was a nameplate only, the website was a shell, there were no financials and no activities recorded. The truck had boarded the ship in Santander, but its journey before that had not yet been traced. The license plates were ostensibly Spanish but had been found to be fake.

The stated destination for the truck, according to the fake manifest, was the non-existent address near Liverpool city centre, which had been confirmed by Stuart. For Darren this meant it was clear that the truck was never meant to arrive anywhere; it pointed to murder. Why was no-one else keen to pick up on this? They were more concerned with how the truck had been released from the ship in the first place. Port Police had a lot of explaining to do.

As the updates continued, pathology confirmed from their

feet that the bodies in the truck were those of eight men, between the ages of twenty and forty, ethnically European. Interpol were checking through European missing persons, but it was like searching for a needle in a haystack. Fire investigations, reported Matt, were so far inconclusive, and pointed to poor truck maintenance. The fire had started in the cab, which suggested an electrical fault that had then spread to the engine. There was still no explanation for why the men's feet didn't incinerate.

But Darren was struggling to concentrate, because something was distracting him. The word 'Grannus.' Where had he heard it before? As the meeting began to wrap up with tasks being assigned for the day, he surreptitiously typed the word into his phone under the table. *Grannus. In the Celtic polytheism of classical antiquity, Grannus was a deity associated with spas, healing and mineral springs…* Those chalets in Les Paons….Darren remembered tramping through the grass as Helen pointed out to him the names of chalets: Luxtos, Lenus, Grannus… it wasn't the Kuper chalet, it was another one, but this had to mean something. It couldn't possibly be coincidence, could it? Darren felt jolts of electricity and adrenalin through his body. He could hear the blood coursing through his veins, he turned in on himself, and as the meeting went on, the voices on the outside were as if underwater.

And his excitement was tinged with guilt and frustration, because he was going off on a tangent; he was on a path that he felt he couldn't leave, yet it was impossible to explain it to anyone. A logistics firm called Grannus owned a truck containing illegal male workers; for Darren this meant that the construction industry must surely be the key. And there was one player who had a virtual monopoly on the local construction industry.

'What's the plan for today, boss? Shall we bring in Val Killy now?'
'Yeah, straight away. This is big.' Back in their cubicle, Darren stood at the whiteboard listing the tasks for the day.

He looked at his watch, and said, 'She'll probably be at work in Foxy Ladies by now, and that's only round the corner from here so it won't take long to find her. Colette, do you think you can handle her initial questioning? Dave you can sit in. And Baz, please follow up with the fire teams in Crosby village.'

Colette looked confused. 'Boss, that's fine, but what are you doing if you're not questioning Val?'

'I'll be back soon. I'm going to visit a few construction firms first,' he added, apropos of nothing.

'What for boss? Isn't that off-remit?'

'As far as I'm concerned it's directly on remit. If those men that died were construction workers, then this whole thing might have been a set-up by one of the players in the industry, to destroy a rival. We need to look into working practices, management structures, people who might have some beef with Max Killy.'

'You'd better not visit Shawn Forrest though,' said Colette. 'City council golden boy? Canter would go mad! He's definitely not involved.'

'No, I'll steer clear of him.'

But Colette was still looking at Darren. He knew that she was questioning his judgement, and not for the first time. But she had trusted him before and it had led them to killers. He wished he could tell her... but that would be crazy. Two cases, two potentially supernatural elements that went against everything he believed in but which he simply couldn't ignore.

As he headed for the door, Colette ventured, 'Boss, did you ever think that the Crosby village fire might be just an unexplained death?'

He paused for a moment. 'Well, it's our job to help prove that it was or wasn't.'

A part of Darren secretly hoped that the pathologist's outcome would not be unexplained death. Because once that went to the coroner, then his role in the case would be over. Evidence of foul play would allow him to keep investigating.

104

***

Darren parked at the Albert Dock and walked over to the Lumina 2 construction site, where Forrest Plc had its temporary yet luxurious site office.

In this epicentre of modern Liverpool, the past was locked in a turbulent battle with the future: the eighteenth century dock buildings behind him and the cathedrals piercing the horizon in front; the old streets of Toxteth to his right and cavernous warehouses that had been turned into bowling alleys and conference centres. A hundred metres down the road Lumina 1 glittered preposterously in the sunlight, so sparkling it was impossible to look at directly, like the sun. The glare helped to disguise the 'To Let' signs that betrayed vacant units inside.

In front of Darren, Lumina 2 was almost the same height as its sister or brother tower, but it was still just a framework of scaffolding, swathed in the green construction wrapping of Forrest Group. This sheeting blocked out the light, providing merciful shade as Darren approached. The word Forrest was imprinted a hundred times around the synthetic sheeting, which fluttered in the ever so slight breeze that caught it occasionally. The site appeared to be deserted.

Just six years before, Shawn Forrest was in prison beginning a fifteen-year sentence for racketeering, fraud and money laundering, a string of unproven armed robberies and drug deals connected to his name. With a network like his, prison would have been no barrier to the continuance of his business, but he decided to make a remarkable about-turn. In a spectacular return to grace he managed to secure his early release through turning informant, cutting a deal with the Crown Prosecution Service and working with the police to dismantle criminal networks across the country. This was the platform on which he built his new reputation, and he not only earned himself a pardon but was given the claim publicly of having single-handedly destroyed the Liverpool drugs trade. This of course had the added bonus of enabling him to take revenge upon his enemies.

Forrest didn't stop there. He became religious in prison, finding God, returning to his Catholic roots and becoming devout. He taught and preached to prisoners, writing a self-help book and convincing the world that he had seen the light and turned over a new leaf. And rather than head for comfortable retirement on the Costa del Sol, he was drawn back inexorably to his home town, where he still needed to be a figurehead, this time of the angelic sort rather than the anti-hero sort. Most of the city of Liverpool appeared to have accepted him back and forgiven his past. But in his natural cynicism, Darren felt that people didn't know, or didn't believe, the extent of Forrest's former brutality. He himself couldn't believe that someone who he had been capable of applying blow-torches to his rivals' genitals could possibly change. At the same time, no matter how evil Forrest's past crime, he was not prepared to let Max Killy loose on him to take vigilante revenge; there had been enough cross-fire casualties already.

The air-conditioned site office was designed as a show-home, with low, neutral-toned furniture, shiny units and glossy brochures. Darren rang the buzzer and entered, and there was Shawn Forrest at the desk, surprisingly accessible, leaning back in his chair on his mobile phone. He ended the call when he saw Darren, and stood up.

Forrest was undoubtedly handsome, approaching middle-age but appearing younger. There was not a wrinkle on his skin, only the scar that ran down the side of one cheek, an ineradicable reminder of his violent past.

'Hello, Mr. Forrest, I'm Detective Inspector Darren Swift from the Major Incident Team,' Darren stepped forward to shake hands. 'I'm just here to ask you a few questions, information gathering really, in relation to the truck fire the other day.'

Forrest shook his head vigorously as he motioned for Darren to sit.

'Terrible, terrible thing. Not something a city could ever be prepared for, especially one as welcoming as ours. I'm helping to organise a vigil for the victims this Friday. I hope the police will attend. To show that the men won't be forgotten, that the city cares.'

'I don't think there's any doubt that the city cares, Mr Forrest. So that event will be sponsored by Forrest Group then will it? On the news?'

Forrest smiled. 'I know what you're getting at, Detective. I know I have my critics, especially amongst your good selves, the police. And to be fair, you have your reasons. I was a bad lad once. But I've changed. You may not believe me, but it is true. Liverpool loves a local hero. They need it.'

Darren hated the way he referred to Liverpool in such a paternalistic way. When Forrest spoke he used the same over-enunciation and carefully chosen sophisticated words as Max Killy, yet he did it with more grace. Forrest's accent was soft; he had made a concerted effort to lose it as part of his reinvention as a businessman.

'Mr Forrest, tell me about your employees. If we were to look at the human resources of Forrest Group, what would we see?'

'By that I assume you're interested in my construction workers? Because Forrest Group has nothing to do with the truck fire.'

Darren ignored him. 'How many construction employees do you have Mr Forrest?'

'Well, that's a very difficult question to answer at any one time. It varies according to the jobs we've got going on. We try to employ local where we can, but I'd say around fifty per cent of our employees come from eastern Europe and the Baltic – all on EU passports through agencies. All above board, with documentation to prove it. Not a single illegal, I can assure you. You have my word.'

'Right, OK. We can check all that anyway, as you say. Lumina went up very quickly, didn't it? This time last year it was a car park.'

'We had a lot of support from the city council. Fortunately, they share my vision for the future of Liverpool.'

'And what's that? Private sector investment, corporate buy-outs of local businesses?'

'Look, Detective Swift. God knows I love scousers. I am one of them. I wouldn't be here if my heart wasn't here. I'm bonded to this place, I can't leave. But scousers don't always know what's good for them. It's the council's willingness to engage with private sector investment that will take this city forward. The government abandoned us in the Eighties. 'Managed decline', they called it. I was there, in Toxteth, when the country cast us off, when Thatcher left us to rot. Now we need to be a mini-state of our own.'

Darren winced internally at Forrest's patronisation of his people, his city, but he had to admit to there being a grain of truth in it. Occasionally Liverpudlians could be their own worst enemies. But the city's success certainly had very little to do with the UK government. It had been managed locally, with the help of the European Union, and underpinned by the Scouse spirit of enterprise, openness and courage. What's more, Darren didn't agree that Forrest's vision of a prosperous Liverpool included everyone. Thanks to government austerity, the gap between rich and poor in the northwest had never been greater, and Darren felt that the last type of hero the city needed was one with expensive cars and watches.

Darren thought he would never get over his scepticism about Forrest's reinvention as a local hero. It surprised him how selectively short people's memories could be, when it suited them. Ten years ago Forrest was regularly torturing rival drug dealers, and although it was unproven he had likely ordered the murder of several. He seemed to have arranged a press injunction on the more unsavoury aspects of his past, and had used a PR firm to paint a media picture of his life as a rags-to-riches tale, him as a family man who went to church every Sunday.

'So what are the names of the employment agencies that you use? And where do you accommodate the foreign workers?'

'I can provide the police with all that information, Detective, no problem. I can have all the books ready for you within a few hours, but as you see this is just a temporary site office.'

'Ever have any run-ins with Max Killy?'

Forrest nodded, amused. 'Who hasn't? We had a few issues about eighteen months ago with his heavies asking for protection money; nothing we couldn't handle. But he is not really involved in the construction industry is he? I think the glory days of Liverpool organised crime are over now.'

'Come on, Mr Forrest, we both know that's not true.'

Forrest smiled questioningly. 'Well, I wouldn't know.'

Darren paused and pretended to look at his notes.

'You know Thomas Kuper, don't you?'

'Yes, quite well. You could say we're business partners. He owns a couple of units in Lumina, and he's thinking about buying a share of Lumina 2. We also do charity work together. He'll be at the vigil tomorrow, of course.'

Darren gestured to the green structure outside.

'How is Lumina 2 going? Sold all the units yet?'

'No, not yet. Are you interested for yourself, Detective? We have some very nice apartments—'

'Bit out of my price range I'm afraid. Looks very quiet on the site today.'

'You think I would allow people to work in this heat? It's a furnace in there, under those canvasses. I protect my workers and it's far too hot to do manual labour in this weather. Look, it's a terrible thing, but I'm sorry I don't think I can help you with the truck.'

'Do you know anyone operating in the north-west who doesn't protect their workers? Who doesn't have your ethical practices?'

'There are plenty of unscrupulous construction firms, that's well known. But around here? No, I can't think.'

'In any case, you have a monopoly on all the big projects though, right?'

Forrest opened his mouth to speak, and then stopped and smiled knowingly.

'I accept your hostility, Detective. But you will find there's nothing to concern yourself with here.'

He stood up, and Darren felt himself being ushered out.

'Here, take one of our brochures.' Forrest handed him one, then came around the desk and clasped his hand firmly, placing the other on his back to steer him towards the door. 'And I do hope you will come to the vigil tomorrow night.'

Stepping out into the blazing heat reminded Darren how beautifully air-conditioned that temporary office had been. His skin began to perspire immediately, and he was blinded by the reflection from the Lumina. It really was an absurd building, he thought. He made for the shade of the building site fence, and leafed through the brochure as he walked back to the car, as slowly as possible to prevent himself from sweating.

Lumina 2 epitomises the future of Liverpool, offering the very apex of modern live-work luxury. Eighty waterfront lofts crowned with eight duplex penthouses offering panoramic views, and underpinned by twenty exciting retail units and 20,000 square feet of contemporary office space. This flagship project, a brother to the glitteringly successful Lumina hotel suite complex, unleashes the full ambition of Forrest Group to have Liverpool live, work and play in the sky.

Darren chucked the glossy brochure in the bin. Before getting into his hot car, he looked around him at the empty construction sites and miscellany of architectures old and new. Liverpool was like a coral reef, beautiful and precarious, teeming with life, teeming with death. Max Killy's words echoed in his thoughts. How would Liverpool fill this number of luxury spaces? Was this real, could this level of rushed development possibly come without a cost? Or were he and Max Killy both living in the past?

***

'Don't you think Darren should be doing this?' said Dave, as he and Colette walked towards the interview room where Val Killy had been installed.

'He trusts us to do a decent job. Anyway, she's not been arrested, we're just questioning her.'

They reached the door of the interview room and Colette took a couple of deep breaths. He's right though, she thought, Darren should be doing this. She herself had plenty of interview experience, but surely this was Detective Inspector territory. Here was a key connection between the two fires, and a golden opportunity to amalgamate their Crosby case with the main investigation, handed to them on a plate by Canter. What was he playing at? He certainly wasn't playing by the rule book, and while she didn't mind that – she loved Darren's creative approach to policing – she did mind that he was shutting her out. He seemed to have an agenda of his own and was making only the most cursory attempts to hide it. Everything about this case made her uncomfortable, from the weird, side-lined remit they'd been given, to the unparalleled horror of the deaths, to the loss of rapport between her and Darren. But here was a chance to make some real progress, even if it led them towards some unpleasant connections with local hero Kuper.

Valerie Killy was a slight but formidable woman, cut from the same cloth as Liz Canter, but born and raised on the other side of the law. She wore a t-shirt that sparkled with the diamante logo of a fashion designer, and more diamonds sparkled on the Rolex watch she wore and frequently touched, as if to remind herself of her good fortune. She sat back in the plastic chair with a fixed expression of studied cynicism and stoic outrage at being dragged in innocent. A classic expression that made no impact on Colette, as she had seen it countless times before on people both innocent and guilty as hell.

Colette and Dave sat across from Val, scraping their chairs under the table, and Colette began recording.

'Interview commenced at 11.15am, present are Detective Constable Col—'

'Have you got a fan?'

'Sorry?'

'An electric fan, you know. It's too hot in here.'

'No, sorry we don't. It's too hot everywhere, I'm afraid.'

Val tutted and shook her head. 'There must be a health and

safety rule about this.'

Colette sighed and continued. These calculated interruptions reminded her of Val's illustrious brother. 'Present are Detective—'

'I want my lawyer.'

'You don't need a solicitor present, this is just questioning.'

The women shot each other daggers that made Dave almost recoil. Colette won the battle and continued, placing in front of Val the photo captured on CCTV at Fones 2 Go.

'Mrs Killy,'

'It's Ms Killy.'

'Ms Killy, you were seen purchasing a mobile phone from the Stanley Road branch of Fones 2 Go on 13th April of this year. That phone was used to telephone your nephew Stuart Killy just seconds before he stopped his truck and exited it, conveniently avoiding an explosion that killed eight people. Why did you call him?'

'I never called him,' she said, aggrieved at the accusation. 'I haven't spoked to Stu since he got out of hospital months ago.'

'But it was your phone.'

'No, it wasn't my phone.'

'Are you denying that you purchased the phone that made that call?'

'No, I'm saying that I didn't make the call.'

'Then who did? Who did you give the phone to?'

'Who did Stuart say it was?'

'He said it was a wrong number.' Colette instantly regretted answering. Val was playing her at her own game.

Val smirked, incurring a wrath in Colette that she rarely felt She slammed her hand down on the table. 'Eight people died and we know you're involved!'

'Look,' conceded Val, 'I'm sure you know that I bought several phones that day from the same shop. No doubt you were going to spring that question on me next. I buy a lot of phones, don't I?'

'So you are stating that you buy burner phones on a

regular basis?'

'Yes! To protect my daughter and her husband! In case you'd forgotten, Detective, my daughter is a celebrity, married to one of the most famous footballers in the world. And I'm not exactly low-profile, with me shop, and me brother. We need to change our phones regularly to protect ourselves. We're fair game for the tabloids, and those phone hackers have got no morals whatsoever, they'll stop at nothing. So we all use unregistered phones in our house, and we change them every few weeks.'

'And have you got anything you need to hide from these tabloids?'

'No! Jesus. Look, it's a matter of privacy. It was the police that advised us to do it, for goodness sake! I'm just trying to protect my daughter. She's very vulnerable.'

Ok, so you buy these phones, give them to Justine and Thomas, and then after a few weeks, then what? Do you discard them?'

'That's what I do with mine. I don't know what they do with theirs.'

'Can you think of any reason why Justine or Thomas might have called Stuart that night?'

'No, none at all. Look, Justine and Thomas probably give those phones away to their friends, so it could have been anyone.'

Colette and Dave looked at each other. Val had outmanoeuvred them. But there was also the possibility that she was telling the truth.

On The Necessary Preparations
For Conjuring Our Lord

Look to the seasons, for these conjurings are best performed when the season is warmed. The hotter the season, the more effective the spell. Consult the almanacks, observe the moveable feasts, consult the prognostications of the astrologers.

Look to the moon, for as the full moon approaches the spell will gain in effectiveness.

Look to the birds, for these are the harbingers of our Lord.

Observe these planetary hours for they are of great importance in performing the various rituals. Failure to observe may make the ritual impotent or cause unwanted effects.

The summer solstice is the optimal moment for the ritual, when the sun is at its highest above the Earth, and the Infinite Flame can be conjured more easily. This is the time for alchemy and necromancy!

It is necessary to be chaste for eight days before these workings, for the lusts of the flesh must be conserved. These bodily desires shall then be cast into the spell. The true follower of our Lord doth not squander his power on base fancies.

The great book must be present. Upon the table you must place the bowl and prepare the candle flame. The image or effigy of thine enemy must be placed in the bowl, and the servant of Adramelech must hold his enemy in his mind and be in communication with him as he recites the conjuration and then says the prayers three times. Note well that the spell

114

is more powerful when thine enemy is present. For if thine enemy doth hear these words, they shall be eightfold more powerful. If thine enemy is not present, hold him well in the mind as the words are recited.

Conjuration:
I conjure thee again, O Lord Adramelech, by all the names of the demons in your service:
Astaroth, Nergal, Baal, Leviathan, Belphegor, Mammon, Anamelech.
Come hither from the Infernal Abodes!

I conjure thee to destroy mine enemy, to let him see what neither God nor Satan hath seen.
This annihilation in thy name. Adramelech.
This annihilation in thy name. Adramelech.
This annihilation in thy name. Adramelech.
This annihilation in thy name. Adramelech.
This annihilation in thy name. Adramelech.
This annihilation in thy name. Adramelech.
This annihilation in thy name. Adramelech.
This annihilation in thy name. Adramelech.

When this conjuration has been said eight times, burn the parchment or effigy with the candle, looking into the flame whilst saying the chosen prayer.

And in this way, thine enemy shall be committed to the roasting place.

1 Ars Adramelechum 2:13

Seven

Helen was in her element again, back at her favourite desk cocooned against the heat inside Liverpool Library. Detached as she was from the immediate horror of the deaths, her head was full of the possibilities of coupe-feu. She treated the practice as a theological conundrum; what if the process was reversed? What if, instead of using this power to quench fire, to stop pain, you could do the opposite? If instead of summoning angels, you summoned demons? Although it was all shrouded in mystery, she had established that the practitioners of coupe-feu appealed to angels, usually one of the three archangels Michael, Gabriel and Raphael. But they somehow combined this with beseeching to pagan deities, usually whichever Celtic deity was most appropriate to the task in hand.

This, in itself, Helen found theologically fascinating, but it was tangential to the task in hand. What if the power of coupe-feu could be used for evil purposes, and what if that was happening in the village? Perhaps one could appeal to Satan instead, or to a demon.

Helen had a copy of Collin de Plancy's *Dictionnaire Infernal*, the nineteenth century encyclopedia of demons, and she was flicking through it with no small amount of horrified glee, poring over the wonderfully grotesque illustrations. Stolas, a demonic crowned owl with long stalking legs, governor of the twenty-six Legions of Spirits, teacher of astronomy, herbs and precious stones. Ipas; Prince of Hell, with the body of a lion, tale of a hare and head of a goose; who knows and can reveal all things, past, present and future. Baal; a duke of sixty-six legions of demons, a deformed cross-breed of a man, cat and toad heads with the legs of a spider, main assistant to Satan.

Each demon had its own sigil, its own powers and areas of interest or speciality. She scrolled through these legions of chthonic deities, enjoying the elaborate, beautiful, shudderingly horrible drawings. This theriomorphy – the manifestation of gods or spirits as animals – was as old as time itself and as new as the werewolves and vampire bats of modern horror stories.

Helen continued to flick backwards and forwards looking for inspiration. She had to admit that most of the texts were so overblown and ridiculous that there was little point in reading them. And then something stopped her – one of the lithographs stood out. This image depicted a sort of anthropomorphic mule; human torso, mule's head and tail; hands behind his back and an expression of absurd pride and snobbery as he displayed the plumed crown on his head, and the full peacock's tail splayed out behind him. *A peacock.* She thought of the electric blue birds that had stalked the garden of Chalet Belenus and that had so unnerved her. And their consorts, the drab female versions of the bird that were pecking at the charred ground of the burnt-out barn.

This was Adramelech, Chancellor of Hell, president of the Devil's general council, keeper of the Devil's wardrobe. In this picture, there was something faintly ridiculous about him, as if the artist was making fun of his pride. But there was nothing funny about the details of this demon. As she continued her research she found that there were various mentions of him in ancient texts, none of them good. He appeared in the Old Testament Book of Kings and in the Talmud as an idol god of the Sepharvaim, a people deported by the Assyrians to Samaria. Adramelech's people were said to worship him by sacrificing children into the fire. Adramelech was also mentioned in Milton's *Paradise Lost* as a fallen angel, and an utterly untrustworthy demon who planned to become more powerful than Satan himself. *A fire demon*, Helen smiled to herself. *Well, well.*

She couldn't help thinking of Mikko, and how he would probably love to write a song about 'this dude.' In fact he probably had already, she thought, and she had a sudden urge to contact him. This was a reason to send him a message perhaps. But more pressing was the question of the village, and about whether there was some connection to Adramelech. This would warrant further research, and she wished she had stayed longer in Les Paons, questioned the old lady more – what would there have been to lose? She did remember that there had been lots of grimoires in that chalet. Grimoire; a type of spell book that was a curiosity of the Middle Ages, popularised during the seventeenth and eighteenth centuries in Europe and then romanticised during the nineteenth century. They were now almost forgotten, locked in the far corners of the occult and the cabalistic. They were like recipe books, filled with strange incantations, markings and diagrams, bastardising Latin and other ancient languages, filled with preposterous rantings inspired by the Bible. Ridiculous, but the word itself – grimoire – was so deliciously evocative of fairy tales and magic that Helen found it irresistible. Often these grimoires were specific to particular types of spell or even to particular angels or demons. What if, she wondered, there was a grimoire especially for Adramelech?

Helen was indeed "going off on one" as she had heard Darren whisper to his boyfriend over the phone, and she was 'totally down for it,' as she imagined Mikko would say. A bit of internet searching confirmed that indeed there was a grimoire for this particular demon: the *Ars Adramelechum*. It was very obscure, very old, and written in French, but there was an English translation from 1879. There was no reference to any later editions printed after 1879, but the existence of this edition itself proved that the book had certainly, at some point, been printed and read in modern times. It didn't seem to exist on Amazon or any of the academic book purchasing sites; in fact not only was it seemingly out of print, it wasn't even mentioned by them. But she found mentions of it on numerous websites – computer games forums, demonic encyclopedias, occult groups – some websites that she quickly clicked away from for fear of their inappropriateness. Gradually she pieced together the fragments of information she could find about the book. It was claimed that an old French translation of the *Ars Adramelechum* had been written, long-hand, in the seventeenth century by a Swiss priest who had travelled to the Middle East and found an ancient Samarian manuscript. He only made two copies, which apparently he bound in human skin. Helen raised her eyebrows at that. She had heard of this practice of anthropodermic bibliopegy as a form of penance for criminal acts in the eighteenth and nineteenth centuries. Convicts facing the gallows, who already knew their bodies were to be 'anatomized' as specimens for medical students, would offer up their skins as a form of atonement. The flesh became a vessel for knowledge and therefore for one's everlasting soul. Helen had always thought this rare and macabre practice was rather romantic, although the thinness of human skin apparently made it very impractical, and she shuddered at the thought of touching one of these books herself.

After these two French copies were apparently made, the trail of the *Ars Adramelechum* went cold until the late nineteenth century when a British scholar from the University of Geneva found one and translated it into English for publication. The fate of the other skin-bound manuscript remained shrouded in mystery.

This was almost certainly going to require a trip to the Bodleian at Oxford University, or the British Library, thought Helen. She simply must get hold of this translation. Liverpool Library was well-stocked, but surely not this well-stocked, they couldn't possibly have something so obscure. But nothing ventured, nothing gained, though, had become her motto, and she went over to the computer terminal to have a cursory look on the library catalogue. And she could hardly believe her luck, because there it was:

Ars Adramalechum, Anon, 1635, transl. W. Lovett 1879, 1st edition

Her heart was beating faster as she bounded over to the reception desk to order up her request. The duty librarian raised her eyebrows comically as she saw Helen approach; they would often joke together about Helen's eccentric reading matter.

'What'll it be this time then love? Angels or demons?'

Helen gave her the reference code and watched expectantly as the librarian typed into the online catalogue, her facial expression turning from optimism to commiseration.

'Sorry love, we actually don't have this one. It says here it was taken out last October, and apparently never returned. I mean, it could be in here somewhere and not have been put back on the system. Things do go walking, you know. But we get the odd theft as well. It's a shame – looks like this was a first edition, probably very valuable. I'll report it on the system.'

Helen could hardly contain her frustration.

'Do you know who borrowed it? Such an obscure thing to choose!'

'I wouldn't be allowed to tell you that, love. Data Protection. But between you and me, I can tell you this – there's nothing down.'

'What do you mean?'

'For some reason the borrower reference has not been entered. Must have been someone new working the system that day. Really disappointing.'

Helen sloped back to her desk deflated. How frustrating, in this day and age, to be unable to find a copy of a book. Nowadays you could find just about anything. And so, how exciting. She resolved to find out as much as she could about this grimoire online, and then perhaps arrange a trip to Oxford or London to procure a copy for herself. It was hard to believe that so-called demonic activities could really be going on in that Swiss village. Nevertheless, she knew this little literary mystery was going to tug at her until she solved it.

The dark house was still stiflingly hot when Darren and Matt returned home from the vigil late that evening and slumped in front of the television. Reporting of the heatwave had become tedious, and the national press and TV channels had leapt upon the Liverpool truck fire as a crystallisation of the tragic plight of immigrants across Europe. So tonight's vigil merited a *Newsnight* special.

The camera panned over thousands of people that packed out the public arena at the Albert Dock in the setting sun, holding banners, carrying teddy bears, flowers. Never Forget. We Will Remember You. The Dock Road Eight. It was hard not to be moved to tears at the city's passion. On a podium illuminated from behind by the setting sun that cast a sparkling pink sheen upon the Lumina, the mayor gave a speech, an appropriately short, clichéd yet moving speech that highlighted Liverpool as multicultural city, that welcomed refugees, that treated everyone as equals, that the victims would not be forgotten. Darren and Matt had both been moved when they stood in the crowd, and they welcomed hearing it again.

But they both bristled and rolled their eyes when the studio analysis began. The talking heads who had been brought in to discuss the event, none of whom were actually from Liverpool, inevitably brought up Hillsborough. It seemed that the rest of the country could barely mention Liverpool in a sentence without Hillsborough – a city in mourning, displays of emotion, and the dog-whistle implication of Scouse histrionics. When in fact all it proved was that now, as then, the city came together in times of trouble. There were a few salient points though, Darren thought. For the example the arrival of illegal immigrants under such terrible conditions showed that despite regeneration, a shiny new mayor and shiny new buildings, the dark underbelly of organised crime was still thriving, hidden just beneath the surface.

And then the discussion turned to Shawn Forrest, and the

camera panned back to the arena. Forrest had taken the podium after the mayor, and given a much longer speech which the news programme elected to broadcast in full. He wore his trademark three-piece suit, and managed to give the impression of not sweating at all. He looked out at the crowd for an exaggerated amount of time, with lips pressed together in anguish, before he finally spoke.

Darren rolled his eyes. 'Get on with it. It's not all about you.'

'Give him a chance, Daz. I think he's great.'

'He's a criminal for God's sake. It was only five years ago he was going round threatening people with a blowtorch.'

'Shut up and listen.'

Forrest began to speak, in his gentrified Scouse tone.

'Fellow citizens, my name is Shawn Forrest and I am a son of this city. I am half-Irish, a quarter American, a quarter English, and one hundred per cent Liverpudlian. I am a son of this city.

'The tragedy that occurred last week on the dock road, in which eight brave men died, touched all of us, because we are a city united. United in grief, united in courage. These eight men may be unidentified, but they are not nameless, for we shall name them. We shall name them sons of Liverpool.'

The camera panned across to a sort of VIP area raised to the side of the podium, where a number of distinguished guests including Thomas and Justine Kuper, and several other footballing couples, stood with heads bowed and hands clasped in front of them. Darren felt that this in itself was inappropriate, to have VIPs at such an event. Surely everyone could see that the speech was too much, that Forrest was hijacking the event for personal gain. But Darren had to admit, it wasn't a bad performance.

Forrest continued. 'As you all know, I didn't use to be the person I am today, and I am grateful to this city for giving me another chance. So now I am repaying my debt. An eye for an eye, as the Bible says.'

Darren snorted. 'Come on, that was a terrible metaphor.'

'Shut up, man, you are really annoying me.' Matt shoved

him.

'Whatever the religion of the deceased, let us all pray together for their souls,' continued Forrest.

'Oh yeah, he went religious in prison didn't he,' said Matt.

'Dear Lord, help us to find and crush the perpetrators of this terrible crime, to meet their fire with our fire. Because fire also comes from heaven.'

Matt said, 'Ok, fine, I admit that was a bit weird.'

As Forrest pronounced these words, the setting sun hit the edge of the Lumina just at the right moment, as if it had been timed to perfection, so that a shaft of gleaming white light escaped from its outer edge and illuminated him from behind.

The news programme returned to the studio, where the discussion turned to the handling of the investigation, and whether the city council was using the truck fire as a convenient smoke screen for municipal problems engendered by the relentless heatwave. *They certainly had a point there*, thought Darren. A pressure cooker was building in the city, which had particularly bad memories of heatwaves. The last time there was such a prolonged heatwave in Liverpool, in the Seventies, water shortages and elderly at risk were not the only problems – the Toxteth riots that decimated the city and left it a national pariah for years were partly to be blamed on weather conditions.

And there was unrest now; everyone could feel it brewing, could feel it in themselves. Lawns were parched, like straw. The men in the truck had become martyrs not just for immigrants but for everyone, the burnt-out truck a metaphor for a city overheating. Old people were beginning to die, hospitals were overrun. Schools were closing as they were too hot for the children; workplaces without air conditioning were shutting down. The atmosphere of this heatwave had changed now. The euphoria had morphed to languidity, had morphed to irritation, had morphed into anxiety, anger. Crosby was only dealing with hosepipe bans, but other parts of the city had bigger problems. The city was a tinder box. But the match would finally be struck in an unlikely place.

Darren turned off the TV and asked Matt about the truck.

'Any developments your end on why the truck caught fire?'

'I knew we should have watched something else! You've still got work in your head! Ok, fine. Look, there are a few reasons why a truck might burn. It's not uncommon, unfortunately. No explosive device has been found, that's pretty clear-cut. So if we're looking at arson, the next step is to find an accelerant. The presence of an accelerant would indicate foul play.'

'Anything detected?'

'Not yet.'

'What kind of an accelerant might it be?'

'Any type of flammable liquid in a place that it shouldn't be. But the problem is that there is of course supposed to be flammable liquid in the truck anyway – the petrol. And from the residues so far nothing abnormal has been picked up. Far more likely is poor maintenance. That is the cause of most truck fires. No specific evidence yet but it was an old truck, and no record of its last maintenance check.'

'So the ultimate owner of the truck would get done for corporate manslaughter. Criminal negligence.'

'Yep, but that's for you lot, not us. We just need to prove what happened. We'll get there.'

'What do you think?'

'Poor maintenance, defo. Which would mean that in a sense, the job you've been given is completely mad. Because what possible connection could there be between the two fires? Other than a weird coincidence? There are fires everywhere right now anyway. It does give you the opportunity to get the Killys once and for all though, doesn't it? To look into the links that are there – the illegal working practices.'

'You would think, wouldn't you? But my hands are tied – I'm only allowed to investigate the connections between the fires themselves. And to be honest, the more I look into this the more I think it's not just about the Killys. I think there might be a bigger player.'

'Who?'

'Forrest.'

'No way! He's a hero!'

'Jesus, that's what everyone says. A leopard doesn't change his spots, isn't that what they also say? Anyway look, I'm not saying he's even involved, but he might be a target. And someone like Forrest won't go down without taking a lot of bodies with him.'

'Maybe. I suppose there could be a new sort of gang warfare going on in the construction industry, and he could be a target. Right, I'm going to bed.'

'I'll be up in a minute,' said Darren, moving to the kitchen table to check his email.

'No you won't. It's alright.' Matt went over and massaged his shoulders, feeling the knots of tension. 'I know you're not avoiding me. But these dreams… you could see someone, you know. It's OK to say that a case has affected you. That's what police counsellors are there for.'

'I'm fine about the Shepherd case, honest. It hasn't affected me,' Darren lied, because the images that haunted him at night were of wrought iron gates, immiscible skies, and the souls of babies.

'I'm not just talking about the Shepherd case. You should have had counselling after London. You didn't even have a proper debrief, they just shipped you back up here.'

'Yeah, maybe. I'll look into seeing someone.'

'I know you won't.'

'You're right, I won't. But honest to God,' he rested his elbows on the coffee table and rubbed his face with his hands, 'I never thought I'd be afraid of going to sleep.'

'You're just destined to be a troubled soul, you. And I wouldn't have it any other way. I love that furrowed brow of yours. Come on, close that down and let's go to bed.'

Darren was about to obey when his phone rang. He saw that it was Helen.

'I've got to take this, it's work. Honest, I'll be up soon.' Matt wafted a hand at him in mock despair and headed upstairs.

'Hello, Darren, I hope you don't mind me calling so late? I

figured you would be at the vigil until now.'

'Yeah, I was, just got back. Were you there?'

'No, I'm afraid I got very side-tracked this evening. I know this is still utterly frivolous, but seeing as we've come this far I thought I should tell you what I've found out. It's quite fascinating. Quite ominous as well, I suppose. If... well, anyway...'

Darren laughed at her endearing gaucheness. 'Go on then, let's hear it.' And he did really want to hear it.

'Well, it's about the peacocks, actually. I should have known this before, I'm kicking myself, but I suppose I'm more of an expert on angels than demons. Anyway, I was looking through one of the books I took out about... well, about all this occultism. I suppose I was looking for evidence about demon-summoning, but it was just rather fun really. So... you know we saw all those peacocks in the village? Well, it turns out that the peacock is the symbol of Adramelech.'

'What's that?'

'Adramelech. In mythology he's a demon. Sorry, that's very sexist of me – it's a demon. The demon most commonly associated with fire. It often takes the form of a peacock, according to various encyclopedias I looked at. And it did make me wonder about all those peacocks in the village, particularly because it's called Les Paons. Les Paons means 'peacocks' in French for goodness' sake, we didn't even realise! So I did a little more digging. Firstly, about those newspaper cases reporting the village cult – well, the villagers of Les Paons were accused by a priest ten years ago of worshipping fire demons. I suppose that's why they were so unfriendly there, since they have been given such a bad reputation by outsiders.

'Secondly, the most important text on Adramelech is the *Ars Adramelechum*, a seventeenth century grimoire that was written – you've guessed it – in the Jura region of Switzerland. I'm sure it must be connected with the village of Les Paons.'

As she spoke, Darren had been typing 'Adramelech' in to

his search engine, trying to figure out how to spell it, and his screen was now filled with images of fiery demons.

'Hold on. What's a grimoire?'

'It's a sort of magical textbook, with sets of instructions for summoning demons. Now here's the most interesting part, Darren. I went to the library to see if by chance they had a copy. There was an English translation written in 1879. Liverpool Library is not the biggest library in the world by any means, but it's pretty well-stocked, particularly with theology books. And lo and behold they did have a copy, but it was borrowed anonymously last October, and never returned. Someone in Liverpool has been reading it!'

Darren's mind was swimming, as he tried to establish with what level of cynicism he should evaluate this information. Someone in Liverpool had been reading about how to summon demons that cause fire. On one level it sort of made sense to him, on another it was completely ludicrous. He was going against all his own rules and could never mention any of this to his team. But Helen was still talking.

'So Darren, that means I don't actually have a copy of the book, but I did find a few excerpts online, on some very odd websites. Some of them quite nasty websites really. It's a terrible book, or a terrible translation anyway. This William Lovett, the Victorian translator, appears to have been quite a pompous and tedious fellow, and his writing is a melange of pastiche and melodrama. I do wonder if he made it up himself entirely, as a sort of hokey parody of the Bible. This was around the time when 'found texts' were very fashionable in Victorian gothic literature, and it was quite common to invent them, although it was usually done openly as part of a novel. Anyway, it seems that this poor bloke met with a bitter end. He didn't publish anything else after this and appears to have become an opium addict and eventually died in a fire. I will try and get hold of a copy of this book, but it's certainly not available on the internet. It doesn't seem to be in the British Library either.'

There was an awkward silence on the phone, because Darren had no idea what to say. What could he possibly do with this information? Helen finally broke the silence. She seemed embarrassed at having talked so much.

'Well, it's very late. I suppose I'll go now. I… oh, there's something else.'

'Go on.'

'Belenus, that's it. Chalet Belenus, do you remember, it was the name of the Kuper family home in Les Paons and I couldn't remember what it meant? Well, I looked it up. Belenus is the Celtic god of fire.'

'God of fire, right.'

'Yes. Well, good night Darren. Sleep well.'

'Yeah, you too. Bye, Helen, bye now,' he said distractedly. And then he jumped, because he realised that Matt was leaning over the kitchen counter looking at his computer screen, which was filled with images of fiery demons. He had come downstairs to get a drink of water, and moved noiselessly into the kitchen. Darren hated how he did that. The more secretive he became, the more irritated he became by the person he loved. It was too late to clear his screen.

'Sister Helen, eh? And fiery demons? What the hell are you doing, Darren? Turn that off and come to bed.'

On Numbers

Mark ye well the number Eight!
  For the Number of Our Lord shall be Eight!
  Eight is the number of perfection, of infinity. It doth correspond to the eternal order, the final point of the manifestation, the totality of the universe.

Yea, his number shall be Eight!
  For Eight Thousand years he fell!
  For Eight Thousand years he recovered!
  Eight is the Great Tetrachtys, the lemniscate, the ourobouros, the analemma, the octave.

Verily his number shall be Eight!
  For Eight Thousand years he served and plotted!
  And when Our Lord returns He shall have Eight commanders of his army on Earth, this army being made of Eight Hundred Thousand men!

Adramelech was the eighth archangel. Banished, he will come to take his revenge!
  The octave is the eighth note that begins the musical cycle anew on a higher level.
  The eight-pointed star is the morning and evening star, the goddess Inanna of the Sumerians, the creator of wisdom, the queen of Earth and Heaven.

Place under the sign of Eight the one who is to be born again.
  For this number represents the earth, not in its surface but in its volume, since eight is the first cubic number after one.

It therefore represents all the dimensions of heaven, hell and the infinite space, in their totality.

Mark ye well the number Eight! For when ye see this number, there ye shall find Adramelech!

1 Ars Adramelechum 2:13

Eight

Nine o'clock in the morning in the incident room at Canning Place, and the whir of fans produced a constellation of competing warm winds that stirred the beige room. Combined with the anxious humming of an overloaded air-conditioning system and the incessant ringing of phones, it was difficult to hear anything over the level of white noise.

Walking through the desks in the open-plan office, Darren tried to put all thoughts of demons out of his mind. It wasn't as if he could discuss them with anyone. And in any case, back in reality, there were plenty of other troubling aspects to this case. From Darren's perspective, the multi-agency approach was not working as it should. All the right agencies were involved, but only to the extent of information-sharing, platitudes and commiserations. The focus continued to be on forensics, on establishing the technical cause of the truck fire, while making statements from the side-lines about how terrible it was for illegal immigrants. The real opportunity here, to delve deep into human trafficking in the northwest, into exploitative labour practices, was being missed, and Darren felt he knew why. Canter was being blocked, he knew it. Someone high up in the city council was whispering in her ear, someone who was protecting Shawn Forrest's business interests. Because any clampdown on local labour practices would slow down his work and damage his profits. It didn't make any sense otherwise. And it wasn't correct. Darren was starting to believe, with a not inconsiderable amount of chagrin, that Max Killy might have it right.

'Convoluted supply chains and subcontracting'; that was what Dr Hassan had said. And surely that was what they should be investigating. He was sure his team would be with

131

him. And if he was going to be blocked from official channels, he would go unofficial on them. Starting with that mystery driver who had disappeared into the ether, into the dark crevices between the containers. DCI McGregor would be looking for the driver himself, of course, but Darren thought he could do a better job. The docks. Darren knew them like the back of his hand; he had grown up there, gazing from the top deck of the bus at the ranges of coloured containers, eager to see what cargoes had been unloaded that day. A row of twenty stretch-limo jeeps, gleaming white. An army of brand new yellow backhoe loaders, delivered from Japan; a line of green combine harvesters, a feast for a little boy's eyes. He had never lost this childish wonder for the docks and still looked every time, taking in the shifting movements of this busy concrete plain.

It was bizarre that none of the CCTV cameras that were ubiquitous in the area had captured the missing driver. How had he slipped through? His evasion of cameras implied that the escape was orchestrated by someone who knew the docks even better than Darren. It pointed to an inside job, or to someone like Darren who had grown up there.

Where would I go? If it was me, where would I hide?

The docks were filled with nooks and crannies, but they were also filled with CCTV cameras. The glory days of the Seventies and Eighties, when there had been little difference between dock workers, truck drivers and criminals as they walked off with the pick of whatever they wanted, those days were long gone. Although fondly remembered by those such as Max Killy.

Darren closed the glass door into the relative quiet of his team's office space. Three pairs of eyes looked up apprehensively.

'Canter's on the warpath, Boss,' said Colette. 'She wants to see you in her office. Apparently Shawn Forrest has made a complaint.'

'Shit. Right, I'll be back in a bit.'

He made moves to leave, but Colette stopped him.

'Wait. Before you go, there's been a development. Val Killy went in to Copy Lane police station early this morning and asked to change her statement. She now says that Eliza Bektashi approached her via an ad she placed in the local paper, and was not hired via an agency.'

Darren nodded. 'Therefore, not through her brother. No doubt Max leaned on her. That's no surprise. But it might be true though. Let's go back and take new statements from the lot of them. She's already in a lot of trouble for hiring someone illegally, so we might be able to get more out of her. Maybe she'll change her story on the phones as well.'

He headed over to Canter's glass-fronted office, outside of which there was a ragged queue of people needing to speak to her. When she saw Darren she stood up and motioned for him to come through. He closed the door and sat opposite her.

'I feel like we've had this conversation before, Darren. Questioning Shawn Forrest? What the actual fuck were you thinking? The last thing I need right now is the Mayor's office or the Police Commissioner leaning on me. I gave you a very clear remit, and it did not include construction.'

'I don't get it. He doesn't have the right to complain about being questioned.'

'Perhaps I wasn't clear enough, Darren. Shawn Forrest is not part of your investigation. The city's economy and reputation are on the line again, and he's an integral part of that. We need him on side. Look, if the coroner's verdict on Eliza Bektashi comes back as unexplained death, your part of this case is closed. There's no link then. Which works out well, because now we've got an October date for the Andrew Shepherd case – so you'll need to get back on documentation as soon as possible. You're the Officer In The Case, it's a big job.'

They looked at each other, and Canter sighed. 'You know how it is, Darren. Since the government cuts my hands are tied; Merseyside Police are beholden to the city council for funding. And the city council are beholden to corporate investors. So we can't go around pissing them off, without evidence.'

'There's a whole investigation going on into Forrest's financial irregularities!'

'But that's completely separate from this case! There's absolutely nothing to tie Forrest Group to the truck fire. Look, I know you were just information-gathering. But I'm walking on a tightrope here. Plus, I imagine you were your usual charming self, which won't have gone down well. Cultivate your mean and moody reputation with someone else. For my sake.'

Darren felt curiously detached from this telling off, and as the atmosphere calmed down and he and Canter updated each other on the rest of the case, and discussed the latest means by which the Conservative government had screwed Liverpool, he was on autopilot. For Darren's investigation had long taken on a life of its own, which could never be true police work. Yet again, Darren was being drawn into a realm that was not his, and yet which held an irresistible pull.

Just before he began his police training, in a last-chance opportunity to assuage his curiosity, he had taken an ecstasy tablet one night. Nineties rave culture was over by then, but it never really died in Liverpool and the joy of ending the evening in a cavernous, anonymous warehouse engulfed in beats and basslines was still going strong. Indeed, Liverpool had always added an extra glamour to the scene all of its own, and with drug culture lagging behind the south of the country, ecstasy was late to arrive and still the drug of choice in the Noughties. Although most of his friends had taken the pills countless times, Darren was still scared; he knew the horror stories and that there was always the chance you would be one of them. His upbringing had schooled him to be afraid of everything, and in particular of things like this. His friends told him to be aware of the paranoia that would come, and he awaited it with no expectation of pleasure whatsoever. So nothing could have prepared him for the pure feelings that unfolded inside him as the drug took hold, like a flower blooming without end. Now he understood the music; now he understood what he was feeling, what other people were feeling; now he understood everything.

He looked at himself in the nightclub's bathroom mirror, in slow wonderment at the blackness of his dilated pupils. The muffled beats from the dancefloor outside seemed to be at one with his heartbeat, and he became exquisitely aware of his place in the universe. He was no-one and everyone, the earth was the centre of the universe and at the same time a tiny insignificant speck upon it. Most importantly he became keenly aware that there were infinite worlds out there, even inside his own mind, infinite dimensions that would never be discovered, and that he should never be afraid. Just knowing they were there was everything, and there was no fear to be detected in this incalculably pleasurable crisis of ontology.

The following day as he wandered around in blank wakeful exhaustion, unlike after a night of heavy drinking when all was a paranoid blur, he had found himself keenly able to remember every moment of the night before, to dial up those feelings and enjoy them and contemplate them again. It was fascinating, and completely unaddictive. He had no desire whatsoever to take the drug again, because what had been unlocked would remain unlocked forever. Or perhaps he was afraid to go further down this path for fear of what else he might discover, out of fear that the mundane, the everyday, would no longer be enough.

But in the days and weeks that followed, as the memory of the drug faded, he couldn't help but notice that the real world was somehow less colourful than before. The brightness had faded, ever so slightly; everything was now as a sepia-toned photograph, lacking in vivacity.

And so although a part of him was eager to recreate those feelings, he resisted for fear that after the second time the world would be even less colourful than before.

He had had a similar feeling – no, less than a feeling, for he could barely describe it – since the Shepherd case; as if he had been given a glimpse of something so otherworldly, that the ordinary world was no longer enough, no longer seemed important. He couldn't shake the feeling that reality was just like the sweaty sheen of sun lotion on Scouse skin; and that underneath the pockmarks and freckles and tattoos was something infinite and infinitely more terrifying. He had been given a peek at the potential other dimensions, and perhaps the mundane was not enough for him anymore. The detective work that had inspired and thrilled him before was now as nothing, because he had caught sight of a very different sort of good and evil.

When he returned to his team's cubicle, he could sense immediately that there was an atmosphere, and that they had been talking about him.

'Out with it then,' he said. 'What's going on?'

Dave sighed. 'I'm not being funny but, why did you visit Forrest without telling us?'

Darren couldn't help jumping to indignation. 'I just don't understand why you're all hero-worshipping Shawn Forrest! It's like you've forgotten all those crimes he committed.'

'People can change, Darren. People can turn over a new leaf. Maybe he deserves a second chance. Look what he's done for the city.'

Colette added, with a bitterness he had never heard in her before, 'And anyway, Darren, you're not averse to a bit of hero-worship yourself, are you?'

'What d'you mean?'

'Thomas Kuper of course. The sun doesn't shine out of his arse either, you know. It's like you've forgotten about those domestic violence rumours.'

'There's no way that's true. No way. It was a total myth, made up on social media.'

'Well. Just saying. Anyway, the point is, you deliberately kept us in the dark.'

Baz finally spoke. He was the quietest of the team, but once in a while came out with something that encapsulated what they were all thinking.

'To be honest, boss, we don't know what we're even doing here… it feels like a road to nowhere. I mean, obviously it's a privilege to be seconded here to headquarters and whatnot. But – and I hope you don't mind me saying – it feels as if you've been side-lined a bit. Like you've not really been given anything to investigate.'

Darren knew he was right. This co-ordination role was bullshit. He wished he could tell them about Switzerland. But he couldn't, not without destroying the last vestiges of respect they might have for his detective skills. He was now conducting two parallel investigations, one of them completely off-grid and possibly completely insane. He decided to continue playing the indignant card.

'Right, I'm going to question Val Killy again. Is that alright with yous?' He slammed the door as he left.

On The Companion Of Our Lord Adramelech

And it is told that Satan in his generosity provided the Lord Adramelech with a companion for his base requirements and pleasures. And her name was Anamelech. As Adramelech takes the form of a peacock, his consort takes that of a quail or pheasant.

Now this Anamelech bore him a child, and this child was foretold to be mightier than all the Kings of the Earth. But the Lord Adramelech was not desirous of a child; he was sorely jealous of the attentions this child received, wanting Anamelech for himself. And then he thought upon the sacrifices he demanded from his followers, and he didst commit his own infant to the flames, to demonstrate the depths of his brutality.

'Mark well my gift to you, my people, for this, this abomination of parental love shall be your only proof. It should be as nothing to you to sacrifice your own. Speak no more then of children, for I shall grant you immortality.'

But Anamelech, who cowered in her quail form while the ritual was being performed, harboured a secret resentment, deep in her bosom. Fie upon he who doth underestimate the wrath of a woman wronged. Fie upon he who doth rip a child from his mother's arms.

Let this be a warning, for it was her Lord himself that didst preach the gospel of revenge.

23 Ars Adramelechum 4:1

138

Nine

Darren rang the doorbell a couple of times, and was about to give up and go and wait in the car when the door finally opened and there was Justine. He had to do a double-take before he recognised her; no make-up, hair tied back, pyjama bottoms, and a cotton vest which only barely covered a bulky maternity bra. She looked like a different person without her eye make-up, and Darren thought she actually looked prettier unkempt. But the slightly sleepy expression remained neutral; she looked utterly unmoved to see the detective back at her doorstep.

'Oh, hello. Me mum's not in, it's just me and the baby. What's it for?'

'Hello, Justine. Sorry to disturb you. I wanted to go over your statement again, since your mum has changed hers. I was hoping to talk to your mum and to Thomas as well. Will they be back soon?'

'What d'you mean?' She said this with an unchanged expression.

'Your mum now says that Eliza didn't come through an agency but that she approached you herself looking for work.'

'Oh right. Well, me mum hired her, so. I don't know. I should know really, shouldn't I?'

Not for the first time, Darren noticed that Justine clearly felt some shame and sadness over Eliza, and wondered if this could be a way in. Unlike her mother's brick wall of a personality, there were cracks here to be opened.

'Do you want to come in then? I've not tidied up.'

They went into the cool house, and Darren saw that the wheels had somewhat come off without Eliza's presence. The lights were switched off and so the house was only dimly lit from the garden patio doors and a skylight over the kitchen. This open-plan kitchen was piled with dishes and Darren could feel by the granular, sticky texture underfoot that the marble floor had not been cleaned. In the living-room area, the baby kicked happily on a gaudy play mat, swiping his little fists at the soft dangling creatures and bells. Baby clothes were strewn on the sofas and Darren had to move aside a changing mat in order to sit down.

'D'you want a drink or…?' It was clear that Justine was not used to playing host by herself, and so Darren politely declined. She knelt on the floor next to the baby, and occasionally her face lit up as she smiled and cooed at him, and each time her sudden expressiveness came as a surprise to Darren.

Darren read out Justine's original statement, which made no mention of Eliza's origins or mode of recruitment whatsoever.

'Are you still happy with that, or do you want to change it?'

'No, that's fine, but maybe I should check with me mum?'

'That's not necessary, it's your statement, not hers. We just need the truth.'

'Ok then.'

Darren wondered if she was in fact vulnerable, this girl. Was she a princess basking in her privilege, or was she also a pawn?

'I saw you at the vigil the other night,' he said. 'You and your husband.'

'Yeah. It was dead sad.'

'Whose idea was it, to go?'

'What d'you mean?'

This is becoming her catchphrase, thought Darren.

'Who decided that you should go?'

'Thomas. I mean, the whole team went.'

'But not your Mum.'

'She was looking after Alfie, wasn't she?'

'Oh yeah.'

He looked out onto the grass where the peacock was, somehow inevitably, stalking.

'That peacock is amazing,' he said, trying to sound enthusiastic. 'Is it a pet?'

'Oh, yeah, I bought it for Thomas as a birthday present last year. He had peacocks in his village in Switzerland, so I thought it would make him feel at home, you know.'

'Beautiful. Do you ever go to visit his home village?'

'He doesn't get much time off. The last time we went was before we got married. In that part of Switzerland apparently you're supposed to go back to your village for six months before you get married, traditionally you know, but he didn't have time for that. We went for a good few weeks though. I was going mad, it was dead boring to be honest. But me mum came as well and we went into Geneva shopping and that.'

'So you know his family then?'

'It's just his grandma now. We need to take the baby over to see her actually. He wants to do the christening there, but me Mum and I want to do a big christening here. Do a magazine deal, like. Christenings are like weddings now in Liverpool, you have big DJs playing and everything.'

'I imagine that will be a huge occasion then.'

'Yeah, probably…' she tailed off. 'Actually, d'you mind just watching the baby for a minute? I've not been to the loo for ages.'

'Er, yeah, OK. I'm not really an expert on babies.'

'He'll just play there, it's alright. Won't be a minute.'

Justine went off upstairs, in no rush at all, Darren thought, and he marvelled slightly at the fact that Justine in her guilelessness, or perhaps something else, had managed to get a policeman, a detective who was ostensibly investigating her, to look after her baby. He knelt down to make some attempt to interact with the baby. Matt had already, very tentatively, brought up the idea of their having children in the near future. His future in-laws had also brought up the idea, less and less tentatively. Darren felt even more awkward interacting with kids than he did with old people, and although he thought he might want to have children himself one day, it was all adding to his sense that everything was happening too soon.

The baby, who had been engrossed in whacking at his coloured mobiles, now noticed Darren's presence and stopped moving. He stared at Darren with bright blue eyes, as if daring him to blink first. That enormous chandelier hung somewhat ominously above their heads, the reflection from its crystals creating a kaleidoscope of colours that twinkled in the baby's eyes. The baby's stare gave Darren the unnerving feeling of being found out. Adding to his discomfort, he noticed that that infernal peacock had come right up to the patio, with its beak almost touching the glass, tail fanned out and quivering, so that both the bird and the baby were staring at him.

He didn't know where to look, so he stood up and went over to peruse the book shelves behind the sofa, Helen having reminded him what an important insight someone's reading matter could be. He could easily tell which section of the shelving was Justine's and which belonged to Thomas. One shelf was half-filled with the pastel-coloured spines of chick-lit novels, propped up at the end by a huge pile of celebrity and fashion magazines. On the shelf underneath was a row of ring-bound folders containing magazine cut-outs. He imagined Val lovingly curating these records of her daughter's career.

At the end of Justine's shelf was a separate pile of four or five well-thumbed, plastic-coated paperbacks with library codes at the base of their spines. These were just generic paperbacks, two that looked like pulp crime thrillers, two with pastel-colours that might be romance or chick lit. But Darren thought of the grimoire that had gone missing from Liverpool Library.

On the next adjoining bookshelf was a row of hard-backed sports biographies, mostly of footballers, including three copies of Thomas' own autobiography, which he'd had ghost-written at the age of twenty-five. Darren hadn't dared to buy a copy for himself for fear of upsetting Matt, and he was tempted to have a peek inside one. The shelves underneath were filled with books in French. Darren couldn't understand what they were but many looked like classic novels. He smiled at the difference in intellect between husband and wife, and then berated himself for his snobbery. Because it was not dissimilar in his own house; Matt was the intellectual one, the bookworm.

Suddenly he was aware of Justine's presence. She was standing on the lower stairs looking at him intently, and for once her eyes were not completely blank, there was a slight questioning in them.

'Has he been alright then?'

'Oh, yeah, not interested in me at all. How often do you go to the library?'

Justine looked bemused so he gestured towards the shelves. 'I was just looking at your books.'

'Oh, those ones are me Mum's; she brings them to read when she's babysitting. She borrows loads and then always forgets to return them. Why d'you ask?'

'No reason. Listen, I'll get out of your way for now. We'll be in touch again to confirm your mum's statement. If you think of anything else, or if Eliza's family, or anyone connected to her, contact the house, please get in touch immediately. When the investigation is over it would be nice to repatriate her remains.'

'What d'you mean?'

'I'll let meself out, don't worry.'

As he closed the front door he heard the crunch of tyres on gravel, and a red Ferrari pulled into the driveway. Thomas Kuper emerged and they looked at each other for a moment, neither able to read the other's expression.

'Hello, Darren. It's been a long time. I hear you're a detective now. Congratulations.'

'Hello, Thomas. Are you playing on Sunday?'

'I hope so, yes. It depends on my knee. We will see. It was… it was terrible, what happened to Eliza. She was a nice lady.'

'Yeah. Nobody deserves to die like that. And we haven't even located her family yet.'

'I wish…' started Thomas. 'I wish… well, I wish it hadn't happened.'

'Well, good luck on Sunday. I'll be there.'

Of Auspices, Augurs and Amulets

Birds shall foretell the coming of our Lord. Take the auspices; be one who observes the activity of birds, for these are omens.

The Oscines shall give auspices by their singing; when the songbirds are silent in summer, so it is time for the coming of our Lord.

The Alites shall give auspices by their flying; when the seabirds come in from the sea and take shelter, so it is time for the coming of our Lord.

The peacocks shall reveal their glorious tails, as a signal that our Lord is watching.

And it is foretold that our Lord Adramelech shall choose the city of birds as his entry and his dwelling on Earth.

Diamond is the chosen jewel of the Lord. For He desires and wants the most precious of materials; He desires and wants to retrieve the pieces of his glorious suit of armour.

And know this: every diamond on the Earth is a fragment of Adramelech's armour, smattered into innumerable pieces on the jagged walls of Purgatory, as He fell from Heaven and was transformed from an Angel into a Beast and didst know great suffering.

And know this: diamonds can only bring pleasure to those with darkness in their hearts, for they are the true people of Adramelech. Whosoever wears diamond out of love is a fool, and shall meet with great suffering.

It is told that there were those amongst the Sepharvites who chose not the way of Adramelech, and these people wore amulets of purple to fend off his power.

He said unto them: 'Purple is mine enemy as is he who wears it. Be warned, o wearers of purple amulets, that I shall be watching and waiting, and when your armour slips so shall I be there.'

24 Ars Adramelechum 7:1

Ten

Derby day, and the city awoke to an electric atmosphere. The pubs began to fill up from mid-morning. There was to be no reprieve from the heat, and local radio stations discussed measures to keep the football fans cool. There had even been mutterings of cancelling, but the city wouldn't hear of it. There would have been uproar.

In Liverpool, you are red or you are blue. In a city of tolerance and fun, when it came to football, everything came second. Anfield and Goodison Park were the two beating hearts of the city, and theirs was the longest-running football rivalry in history, with over two hundred meetings in over one hundred years. Unlike other team rivalries, Liverpool versus Everton was not born out of aggression, territorial claims, politics or class – but out of pure love and passion for football. And more so than with other team rivalries, tragedy and abandonment had frequently brought these two clubs together, so they were experienced at putting their pitch squabbles aside and uniting when it really mattered. But still, the Merseyside derby had seen more red cards than any other fixture in Premier League history, from two-footed lunges to mass brawls as sheer emotion spilled over.

Darren and Matt had both been born red. Their football team was perhaps the only similarity between their childhoods. They had met through football, when the police team played against the fire department, and their fortnightly pilgrimage to the Kop was one of the unshakeable foundations of their relationship. They loved to share the rush of being part of something bigger than themselves, some ephemeral, unspoken power that could easily bring euphoria or misery, to cause a grown man to jump for joy or reduce him to tears. Something that, beneath the salaries and the sponsorship deals, was the essence of humanity.

As they hurried through the turnstiles together, they could already hear the white noise of cheering, some primal drumbeat that was the beating heart of the city. By the time they reached their usual seats, there was a deafening roar, an emotion that you could almost touch, that would bring tears to the eyes even of someone who couldn't possibly understand. The heat was hard to bear, and there was a collective film of sweat-scented humidity, mingled with beer, chips and nicotine, that hung in the air above their heads. Large swathes of the crowd were covered with wafting banners. Out on the pitch, the grass had been perfectly protected from the heatwave, and was just about the only patch of green left in the dried-out city.

The teams ran out to a deafening chorus of *You'll Never Walk Alone*, and then as they stood in lines a hush spontaneously descended over the crowd. There was no need for an announcement; all the city knew there was to be a minute's silence for the Dock Road Eight. Amongst the banners, the red and blue, there were also posters and t-shirts that said 'We Won't Forget You' and similar slogans.

Darren and Matt clasped hands as the silence began. Darren's eyes wandered surreptitiously over to where Thomas Kuper stood at the end of the line, his hands on the shoulders of the young boy mascot in front of him, his lips pressed together in sadness. Kuper was not captain today; he had been given the all-clear to play today, but would probably not be brought on until the last few minutes. Everyone knew this; the minor medical details of footballers made up part of the fabric of daily life. He wasn't an obvious hero – a Swiss peasant wasn't particularly relatable to the Scouse inner-city working class. But his handsome, wiry looks, his shy determination and above all his goal-scoring abilities meant that the city took him in as one of their own. The deal was sealed, of course, when he married local beauty Justine Killy. This adoption of Kuper was a double-edged sword, of course. Because should he ever be sold to another club, or – God forbid – decide to leave himself, the wrath of the city would descend upon him.

Normally a Saturday match was a catharsis for Darren; a safe outpouring of emotion, a chance to share something with Matt, a chance to switch off from detective work, to reconnect with the city, with himself. But today he was struggling to get into the zone, and as the roars washed over him he felt too self-conscious to join in. Something was nagging him, and it was that word: *expendable*. Eliza had been expendable; she had been a warning.

The whistle blew and the cheers, trumpets and drums augmented into a deafening roar again, before settling into a general white noise. Now and again the drone would be punctuated by a recognisable song: the ubiquitous *You'll Never Walk Alone*, or a Beatles song, or a passing fad. Even though he wasn't playing yet, there were plenty of choruses of 'Super Kuper', the Abba track *Super Trouper* which scousers had adapted for their Swiss hero. Suddenly the crowd around Darren erupted so that he was almost lifted off his feet. A goal had already been scored by Liverpool in the third minute. Matt was cheering too, and looked around to see that Darren had not even been watching. Darren tried to look pleased, hated himself for pretending, again, to the person that he loved, and for reasons that he couldn't articulate even to himself.

'Are you alright?'

'Yeah, yeah, sorry. Nice one. I missed it.'

But it was too late to salvage the moment, and Matt's eyes were drawn to where Darren had been looking, over at the Liverpool players' bench where Kuper sat.

'For fuck's sake.'

Darren shook himself and tried to relax, enjoy the atmosphere. But he suddenly noticed that Kuper was looking at his phone. *Don't answer the phone!* That was it! Eliza Bektashi was expendable, yes; but she wasn't a warning. *She was a test run.* The people in front of them were jumping up and down, blocking his view of Kuper, and Darren began to panic. Kuper must not answer the phone. He began to shout, at nothing, and began to push people aside as he manoeuvred his way to the end of the row, from where he ran down the steps towards the pitch. A policeman stepped in front of him. Darren had probably trained this officer at some point.

'I just need to, I just need to…' He ducked and dived to try and see past the uniformed officer who blocked his view.

And then Matt was there behind him. 'Darren, what the fuck are you doing?' He turned him around and shook him around the shoulders, his shout barely audible above the crowd. 'Get a hold of yourself!'

'I need to stop…'

'Come on, let's go.'

'No, I need to—'

'Fuck this. I'm leaving.'

Matt stormed up the gangway steps and looked back at Darren and the pitch, shaking his head before disappearing out of the stands. Darren was ordered back towards his row by the policeman, and he stopped for a few moments to watch Kuper. The footballer spent a few moments typing into his phone, perhaps a text message or a tweet, and then he was nudged by the coach next to him, put his phone away and resumed concentrating on the game. Darren raced up the steps to try and catch up with Matt.

The city was eerily quiet as they made their way home. Everyone was in front of a television screen somewhere, the roads were almost empty, the train carriage almost empty. In silence they looked out of separate windows, Darren at the river, Matt at the city. The argument started up again, as Darren knew it would, when they got out of the station at Waterloo, and they were still arguing when they got home, Matt slamming the door as they stormed into the house.

'I've been patient enough with you Darren, but I'm not a fucking saint. Is there something else you want to tell me?

'What d'you mean?' Darren found himself echoing that idiotic tone of Justine, all the while knowing full well to what Matt was referring, and dreading what was coming next.

'Something about Switzerland? A little weekend getaway?'

Matt had never been angry, bitter, like this before, and he was completely justified. *Why didn't I tell him?* Everything was probably broken now, and Darren wondered, as he had done with his team, if indignation might be a last ditch attempt at salvaging something.

'So you went through my emails?'

'Yeah, because I didn't trust you. And I was right. What the fuck, Darren?'

'It was sort of a work trip. Honestly, it was. But it was last minute, and it was mad, and I didn't know how to tell you, and then... I just left it too late.'

'Look, I still love you, but if you don't want this, I need to know now. Before we both do something we'll regret.'

'I do want this. I love you. It's just... happening too fast.'

And now everything was descending towards a place of annihilation.

***

Dave and Lacey woke almost at the same time, and looked at each other across the tousled sheet. Nobody in the city had used a duvet for weeks. Their eyes sparkled with possibilities, because they were falling in love and they both knew it. On Derby Day the previous day, Lacey had eschewed the usual VIP lunch to which she was always invited as a hanger-on, and at which she always felt second-class and ignored. It was a big step, and she had felt free. Instead she had gone to the pub with Dave and his mates, to watch the big screen television with beers and fish and chips. And for the first time in years she felt herself the centre of attention, important, wanted, special.

Dave, for his part, couldn't quite believe his luck. At one point when Lacey had gone to the bar, his mates looked at her go and said to their friend, 'Fuckin' hell, Dave, you're punching above your weight aren't yer?'

And he had come back with his usual retorts, but inside he glowed with pride.

It was Monday morning and now they would have to drag

themselves to work in the heat, but suddenly everything felt new and for them the heatwave had turned from torpor to romance. Across the debris of Lacey's bedroom was her set of mixing decks and her record collection. She and Dave had discovered they were both budding DJs, Dave more amateurish than Lacey, and he had told her how talented she was and how she should make something more of it, instead of wasting her time working in Foxy Ladies.

'That was the best weekend, honestly,' she said. 'It was so nice just to hang out with your mates. I felt part of it, I haven't felt like that for ages.'

'I know, yeah. I wouldn't even have minded if Liverpool had lost. But 3-0? Nice one.'

'It was meant to be. It was a good day. And Kuper's goal at the end, that was ridiculous.'

'I bet they all had the shags of their lives last night. Apparently they're not allowed to before.'

'I bet Kuper didn't,' said Lacey, her eyes shining with gossip.

'Why not? Oh, I suppose Justine wouldn't be that into it, with the new baby like.'

'She never really was. Kuper was her first you know.'

'You're messing!'

'He was, honestly! She was a good girl at school, just wasn't that into it. And that's part of the problem; she didn't get it out of her system before she got married. And now, Thomas isn't that into it either.'

'What, you think he's getting it elsewhere? Having an affair?'

'Nope.'

'Oh, is he gay?'

'Maybe. But I think he might be one of those… asexuals. He's just not into it.'

'That's sad that is.'

'Maybe not. Kuper has a quiet life, and Justine is getting some elsewhere.'

'Elsewhere? She's the one having an affair?'

Lacey's eyes flashed with mischievous knowledge again,

and Dave asked, 'Go on, who with?'

'You know that Shawn Forrest?'

'Fuckin' hell. Really?'

Lacey nodded and raised her eyebrows. Dave flung himself onto his back, shaking his head.

'What first attracted you to the violent psychopath Shawn Forrest? Jesus.'

He looked up at the ceiling, his mind whirring. That's why Justine hadn't spoken to her husband the entire evening at the Lumina. She was avoiding contact with Forrest, the person with whom she was having an affair. Lacey could see that his mind was racing, and suddenly remembered that she was dating a policeman.

'Oh shit, Dave, don't tell anyone. You can't tell the police.'

With a flicker of hesitation, he said 'Nah, course not, don't worry. Nothing to do with them. And now,' he rolled on top of her and kissed her neck, making her squeal with laughter, 'now I shall make you Dave's famous Monday morning breakfast.'

He jumped out of bed, wanting to get away from his lie. The first lie. It was not going to be straightforward. As he cooked, clattering pans and singing cheerfully, he thought and thought. Forrest, Forrest, Forrest. What did this mean? Whatever it meant, Darren needed to know.

***

'Boss, are you in yet?'

'Yeah, just arrived, what is it?'

'I've got something, I'm not sure, but I think it's important. I'm on the train, I'll be there in about ten minutes.'

'OK, nice one.'

Dave had practically jogged to Bootle Oriel Road station that morning, hoping to catch an earlier train, and now he sat on the Mersey Rail Southport line commuter train that rattled its way towards the city centre. Normally he would feel a childish delight at getting a window seat, especially on the western side, overlooking the river. Everybody loved this journey, with the city's industrial history laid out before them; the docks, warehouses, scrapyards, timber yards, and the communities of terraced houses that wove them together. He had loved this journey since he was a little boy, when he would take the train on Saturday mornings with his mother to be dragged around the shops on Church Street and then, if he was lucky, go to Liverpool Museum and McDonalds afterwards. His eyes would dart from sight to sight, captivated by his city as it rushed by. He would gaze in wonder and trepidation at the Kingsway tunnel vent, the 1970s breezeblock monolith which resembled an alien spaceship landed next to the water, and imagine the feat of civil engineering that dug under the river to the other side. And then when the rattling train suddenly whooshed into the underground and everything went dark he would grab his mother's hand and look at her wide-eyed in excitement.

Nowadays kids weren't bothered about that novelty of whooshing into the tunnel, they were just annoyed that they were losing their phone signal. But today Dave's pupils didn't dart around, they were glazed on the horizon as he tried to figure out what this new piece of information meant. It had to be connected, but how?

Ten minutes later in the office, after Dave had informed the team, Darren had the same expression, staring frantically into space trying to work out what this meant. He looked through the layers of glass, across at Canter, who was in the middle of berating someone who cowered on the other side of her desk. What was she going to make of this?

Colette said, 'So let me get this straight. Justine Kuper, wife of Thomas Kuper and niece of Max Killy, is having an affair with Killy's arch enemy Shawn Forrest. Where does that leave us?'

'It changes everything, but I'm not sure why.' Darren gazed at the whiteboard. 'Is she acting as some sort of industrial spy, for Forrest, or Killy? Does Killy know and is taking revenge? Are they all in on it together?'

'In on what though?'

'God knows. Some sort of trade in illegal workers?'

Dave said, 'Oh yeah, Lacey said something else as well. God, I feel horrible doing this. She reckons that Thomas Kuper knows. About the affair.'

'So why hasn't he done anything about it? Bad publicity for the team?'

'Lacey reckons that Kuper is not interested in women.'

'Oh right. Not easy to be a gay footballer, it's one of the last taboo professions, isn't it?' said Colette, looking at Darren sheepishly. But Dave went on,

'No, actually, Lacey reckons he's not interested in sex at all. You know, asexual or whatever.'

'Anyway, whatever it means,' said Colette, 'it definitely brings Shawn Forrest into the picture, somehow.'

Darren sighed, and opened his hands to his team. He wasn't good at this, but the air needed to be cleared.

'Look, I'm sorry about going to see Forrest behind your backs. It wasn't right of me. It's hard to explain, I just know he's involved somehow – whether he's a victim, criminal – there's something there. My theories are that either he and Killy are in it together, or one of them is trying to frame the other.'

There was an awkward silence, and then Colette said, 'It's alright, boss, we're with you. Just keep us in the loop, and we're a team, yeah?'

There were nods from Dave and Baz. 'So what's the plan then?'

Darren was so energised by the relief of having them back on side that it was hard to contain his enthusiasm. They were on the case again, on the trail of something, and if he could just fix things with Matt tonight, everything would be back on track.

'Right.' He stood up and clapped his hands together. 'So I reckon we'll get nowhere with the company books, with the finances. Forrest is even more lawyered up than Killy. And even if we had access to the finances, we don't have the training to understand them. There's no way we can request an expert; I'm in enough trouble already. I think we should focus on that missing driver. He's the key.'

'But the CCTV has been gone through, there's no trace of him once he left the port.'

'Exactly. So we can use that. We work backwards. It's what we should have done before; it's what we should have done in the Shepherd case.'

'What d'you mean?'

'That whole area is crawling with CCTV cameras. There are hardly any spots not covered. So if he wasn't picked up on camera, then he must have been avoiding them on purpose, and there are very few routes he could have taken. It also means he must have known the area well, or have been well-briefed.'

'What about if he was picked up by a car?'

'Well, we can check. It was late at night, there was hardly any traffic so we can run a check on all vehicles that entered the flyover area during that time.'

'What if he hid out for ages, like under the flyover or something?'

'It's possible. But if he knew what was going to happen, he would have known the area would be crawling with police soon after, he will have needed to get out of there.'

Everyone looked at each other, Darren willing them to be on board.

'Look, I know it's not a perfect plan. But it's a plan. What d'you reckon? That lot,' –he gestured vaguely towards the rest of the Task Force in the office outside – 'are too concerned with targets and figures and media and business. Let's do the police work for them.'

'Alright, nice one. Work backwards.' There was general assent. It would be a huge task to work backwards in this way, but it just might be possible.

The next few hours were spent with heads bent over maps and screens, overlaying possible routes that could have avoided cameras, collating hours of CCTV footage to be fast-forwarded through. It soon became clear that this would take a few days. The team wouldn't need to go back to the area around the docks until they were ready; all of them had known the place since they were children; the streets were a part of them. Darren especially had it imprinted on his memory; every street sign, every door colour.

At the task force morning meeting, things had moved forward considerably. There was now an explanation for the truck fire, the verdict being poor maintenance. Darren flicked through his copy of the report that had been passed around the table, as a fire investigator summarised their findings. Matt wasn't there, and he was on a triple shift so Darren hadn't managed to see him since their fight. Darren's eyes glazed over technical terms and phrases he only half-understood; circuit breaker protection, arc craters, alternator wiring. It appeared that the fire was electrical, starting in the cab, with an arc on the battery cable which had been poorly insulated and fitted with a faulty circuit breaker that had been outlawed ten years ago. In addition, rubs on the fuel lines had resulted in a fuel mist in the engine compartment, hence the rapid explosion. Essentially, Darren understood, it was an old truck that had been poorly maintained. No evidence of tampering or unusual substances had been found, and so the investigation would now move towards assigning responsibility for manslaughter and human trafficking.

As for Eliza Bektashi, the pathologist's final report was back with a verdict of 'unexplained death,' 'with the unverifiable possibilities of acetone or other flammable cleaning product being ignited by a spark.' This would now be submitted to the coroner.

Meanwhile Canter was anxious about the media handling of the case, as the tensions built up in the city. 'I don't need to remind everyone what happened last time Liverpool had a heatwave like this. This case is bringing all sorts of skeletons out of the closet; we've got far right groups knocking about, accusations of this and that from far-left groups. This is a pressure cooker we're in right now, and it could go off any time.'

Basically, thought Darren, both fires now had real-world,

mundane explanations; no conspiracy, no culprits, no murder. His part in this would now be officially over. But Darren was little interested, so keen was he to get back to their new project. 'Official' was no longer relevant to him.

His team were working stealthily, guiltily, without really knowing why. They were off-book, but it felt right, and it was faintly exciting. Occasionally Canter would walk past their cubicle and look through the window to see their heads buried in conversation, fingers pointing at maps and screens. Darren wondered what she thought they were doing; jobsworths pretending to be busy? Dragging out their final report on Eliza Bektashi for as long as possible before they were summoned back to Crosby? He knew she thought his team were a bunch of jokers, and he was starting to wonder whether she didn't think any more highly of him. He was certainly an annoyance to her in this case, and let's face it, what had he actually achieved since being made detective?

But for now he was safe; supposedly side-lined while the task force focused on the supposed real work.

On The Nature Of Power

Know that power begets power. And he that worships the Lord Adramelech shall see his power increase eightfold upon eightfold. With each conjuration, each creature committed to the roasting place, each annihilation in the name of Adramelech, the conjurer shall become stronger.

He who doth perform this rite doth become stronger with each burning. With each victim sacrificed his strength will grow so that the next victim can be greater still. Until the conjurer shall find himself able to annihilate the veritable Kings of the Earth, and take his place in Adramelech's army.

But with this knowledge must come humility; the conjurer must begin in small ways. Indeed, he who doth perform the rites must train himself by building up from the smallest targets. Let not the conjurer lose courage on that account, but exercise these solemn rites and observances with constancy. It is ardently recommended that the conjurer begins his training with small animals. These sacrificial lambs shall be more than expendable.

He can then move on to human specimens, and these shall be known as The Expendable Ones.

He that attempts to destroy his greatest enemies without training shall find himself sorely disappointed, and shall incur the wrath of God, and Satan, and Adramelech. There shall be no hope for this fool. Yet he that trains himself in the manners of destruction with humility, with grace, he shall find that the power of his sorcery shall increase eightfold with each successful incantation. He shall eventually find himself at the right-hand of his Lord Adramelech, and in possession of the deepest secrets of the Infinite Fire.

32 Ars Adramelechum 1.4

Eleven

Two storeys below Hope Street, the lecture theatre was one of the coolest rooms in the city today, and so Helen's seventh lecture in her 'Philosophy of Religion' series was even more well-attended than usual. In her black cotton dress and sandals she felt free; cool air passed between her legs and touched her bare arms as she moved about the stage, and she realised how constraining the nun's habit had been all those years. Not only had it restricted her movement and made her sweat, but she had felt a permanent self-consciousness, playing a role that wasn't really her.

'Last week we discussed the links between religion and morality, and I marked some truly inspired essays, so congratulations, ladies and gentlemen. This week, we are going to come at morality from a different angle; we are going to consider the Problem of Evil. And whether you are religious or not, we all have to face evil in this world.

'As you all know, I used to be, until very recently, a Calvinist nun. And one of the reasons I became a recalcitrant, and eventually fully renounced the Calvinist faith, was the very problem of evil. If God is the author of sin, as Calvinism states, then it is philosophically and morally unacceptable to address the problem of evil. It is just there, not to be questioned, not be considered axiologically. And that was not enough for me.

'So what is evil? Can we define it objectively? Has it always existed? We can think of any number of terrible events that have occurred in human history that we can unequivocally describe as evil. But did the perpetrators, at the time, believe they were committing evil acts? Or did they convince themselves otherwise? Is evil just a matter of point of view? Seldom does anyone admit that they are evil, or even that they have committed evil. As Alexander Solzhenitsyn states in The Gulag Archipelago, "If only it were that easy."

'Let's take, as an example, modern Satanists. They claim to worship Satan, the devil himself, which is surely the very definition of evil. And yet the manifesto of the Church of Satan, as codified in the so-called Satanic Bible, is a list of perfectly reasonably-sounding values – freedom, justice, nobility of thought – nothing apparently wrong with that. And how much harm do they cause? How many Satanists have committed the terrible acts that have been perpetrated in the name of Christianity?'

At this, Helen smiled to herself at the thought of Mikko's death metal band, Total Depravity. Two of his bandmates claimed to be genuine Satan worshippers. One of them had even, somewhat idiotically, had a pentagram tattooed on his forehead. Yet they were two of the nicest and mildest-mannered people she had ever met.

'Some would say, ah, but these are not real Satan worshippers, it's just for show. But if they say they are, who are we to disagree? And if they are not, what does that say about Satan? About God?

'And that takes us to the personification of Satan. Because as modern religions have tended to personify God in human, male human form, Satan also tends to be personified. We do this to help us understand, to relate. Those of you who take my eschatology course will see how human societies have for time immemorial tended to personify death, to help them come to terms with it. Now Satan tends to be personified, not as a human, but as a beast. Theriomorphy – the transformation into beasts – invokes in us an atavistic feeling. The sense of being brought up sharply against something other. The manifestation of the spirit as a beast.'

Behind Helen on the projector she had put up a slide with the image of Escher's 1921 woodcut *The Scapegoat*, showing good and evil as two sides of the same thing. The crosswise symmetry depicted a white goat merged with the likeness of

Christ and a black goat merged with the likeness of Satan. And she thought of Mikko's facetious throwaway observation that 'God and Satan are basically the same dude.'

She noticed, not without some amused self-awareness, that lots of Mikko's ideas were creeping into her lectures and research. That even when she wasn't actively thinking about him, there he was. And to a certain extent she allowed these thoughts to flow unfettered. It was normal, she told herself – he was my first, it never really ended properly, of course he is still in my thoughts. But it would be totally unsuitable to consider anything more. Totally unsuitable.

Nevertheless, her research interests were shifting, away from Christian theology and towards related, but more esoteric subjects: demonology, the occult, the psychology of belief. She was more than half-aware that this was Mikko's influence. She even toyed with the idea of writing a paper on some aspect of heavy metal and religion; she had even made some surreptitious notes on the subject.

As she continued to lecture on different aspects of theriomorphy, she entertained the class with images and tales of the demons about which she had learned. And then she flashed up, simply because he had been on her mind, her new friend Adramelech. The illustration in Colin de Plancy's *Dictionnaire Infernal* made him look faintly ridiculous; more like a Shakespearian comedy character than a fire demon, with his humiliating combination of animal forms and his haughty expression. Helen preferred the scarier looking images from other demonology books and even from computer games that had commandeered Adramelech's identity.

Just as she was about to click on to the next slide, the whole room jumped in fright and turned their heads as there was a bang at the back of the room. The row of small windows at the top of the lecture theatre, which were just above street level, suddenly darkened. A bird – it looked like a pigeon – had somehow smashed into the window, so violently that its remains were splattered against the outer glass, all blood and bones and feathers. And around it, a group of pigeons, perhaps its companions, perhaps eight of them, had landed and lined up along the window ledge. They blocked out the light as they stared into the theatre.

***

By late afternoon that Thursday, Darren and his team had ruled out enough possible routes to give them a reasonable estimate of how the mystery truck driver might have escaped from the port. The four of them assembled underneath the flyover to perform a walk-through of his probable route. They stood around the location where the wire fence had been cut, which had now been fixed.

'So,' said Darren, holding his map. 'He was caught on camera cutting his way out of here at 10.05pm, having taken five minutes to make his way through the port. After that he was not seen on any of the four traffic cams crossing the flyover, which means he has to have gone underneath. If he was picked up there, it would have to have been after 10.30pm, because we've checked every vehicle that came past during those twenty-five minutes and they're all accounted for and clean.

'More likely is that he crossed over to the streets on the other side, and the only route he could have possibly taken after that is there.'

By now they were standing directly underneath the flyover, with the rumble of traffic above them and lorries slowing past them into the port entrance. They looked across to Beacon Street, the only way a runner could possibly have avoided the traffic cams. This street began as rows of terraced houses, tailing off towards warehouses and dereliction at the end.

'There must be fifty residences on that street,' said Colette, hands on her hips, panting in the heat.

'And you know what's at the end of that street don't you. On the other side of those warehouses.'

'Litherland Muscle Gym.'

'Yep. Let's do a little unofficial door-to-door.'

But as they worked their way through the residences, the door-to-door yielded nothing. Nobody seemed suspicious, and even if they did, Darren and his team had no warrant or remit to go investigating. The last few houses before the warehouses, behind which was Litherland Muscle Gym, were uninhabited, plasterboard scrawled with graffiti covering the windows, half the roof tiles lost. The regeneration sweeping the city had not reached this little forgotten corner. But the final house on the left, which also had boards covering the ground floor window, looked as if it might be inhabited. The curtains were drawn back upstairs, there were filled garbage bags in the front porch, and there was a dirty white van parked outside.

'Last try. Come on then. A white van would figure.'

Darren and Colette knocked on the door while the other two waited on the street. Their knocking went unanswered, but there were unmistakeable sounds of life inside; faint voices muttering, a radio or television hastily turned down, footsteps, a chair scraping. The sounds of people wishing not to be found or disturbed. And the smell of cigarette smoke seeping under the front door. So they continued to knock. Darren considered the possibility of calling 'Police, open up!', then decided against it.

'Darren, this door is broken anyway, look.' She waggled the broken door handle, there was indeed no lock there at all.

'Come-ed then. This is well suspicious.'

They pushed the door open and entered a dark narrow hallway with a stairwell. It led through to a smoke-filled kitchen where a group of men were sitting at the table smoking and playing cards. The back door was open. There was a sense of teeming bodies, of too many people, in this small house.

Someone started to descend the staircase, and then ran back up quickly. This alerted the inhabitants of the kitchen who stood up suddenly, their chairs simultaneously scraping on the tiled floor. The man nearest the back door looked Darren in the eye, his expression flashed with fear then he bolted into the garden, slamming the door behind him. His movement, gait and size implied that he was the driver from the CCTV cameras in the port. Darren had watched enough hours of clips of grainy footage to recognise that.

'Hey, stop!'

Darren instinctively ran after him, hurling aside the discarded kitchen chair and opening the back door in time to see the man disappearing over the brick wall at the end of the garden. The man had a head start, but he was small, portly, middle-aged and a smoker; surely, Darren thought, he would have no chance. Plus, Darren knew these streets so well, surely he could cut him off. But with the stakes so high, the man was surprisingly fast. He ran across roads, leaping over barriers and low walls, disappearing down alleys. Whether by chance or design, he was heading for the canal towpath, and Darren slowed down his pursuit for a few seconds to call Dave. There was a chance they could trap him from the other direction. He set off again and heat burned in his chest as he pushed through the pain, using every vestige of his fitness.

Soon Darren emerged on to the towpath, and looked about him to check in which direction the man had headed. In its nineteenth century heyday the Leeds and Liverpool Canal had linked the collieries and textile mills of Bradford and the Wigan coalfield to the port of Liverpool. Nowadays there was no barge traffic of any sort on this stagnant stretch of the canal. The water here was always foul, but in the heatwave it had gradually evaporated into a fetid swamp of grey-brown mud, its dubious treasures revealed: ancient bicycles, car tyres, plastic bags, wrappers of products long discontinued. They poked out of the stinking mud where flies buzzed in the rank early evening air. As well as the man-made debris, there was also a strong sense of organic matter. Dried out snail shells, long pecked clean by birds, scattered the towpath; shrivelled, mangled carcasses of frogs were laid out on the broken paving. A few eels in their last death throes slithered and slapped in the sewage-infused pools, and a lone parched duck staggered forlornly across an abandoned baby's pram that was wedged half-submerged in the stink.

This primordial sludge, these topographies of decay

beneath which lay fathoms of buried tales, reminded Darren of one of his dreams. He shook himself, caught his breath and blocked out the smell as he continued the chase.

The man had turned right down the path towards Bootle, passing under two low bridges which caused Darren to stoop awkwardly to his left as he followed. Darren was gaining on him all the time so that now he could hear the man's panting, see him clutching at his side in pain. It wouldn't be long now, and then here was Dave who appeared in front of him cutting him off in the other direction. The man was trapped, but was still not giving in. He looked about him, from Darren to Dave and back again, and then...

Don't go in the fucking canal, thought Darren.

But he jumped in, heading for the grassy bank on the other side where there was still a possibility of escape. His first foot sank into the sludge up to mid-calf level, and he wobbled but managed to put another foot down and drag the other out so that he was almost mid-way across the grey slime.

For fuck's sake. Darren went in after, sacrificing his brand new Nike trainers in the process. He grabbed him as they reached the grassy bank and they fell down together as the man continued to struggle. This was an absurdly fierce resistance, ultimately futile as Darren pinned him down.

'Who owns that house?' he yelled.

'I don't know, I don't know,' protested the man, speaking with a strong foreign accent, shaking his head. His expression was a mixture of terror and relief.

'Who d'you work for?'

'Grannus. Grannus.'

'What's Grannus? Where do all those men work?'

'Lumina. Lumina work site.'

***

Liz Canter stood alongside Darren, arms folded, looking through the mirrored glass at truck driver Kipras Orentas who sat fidgeting nervously, nursing a coffee, eyes darting around.

'This is a fucking disaster. But OK. It doesn't mean Forrest is guilty of anything at all though.'

Darren rolled his eyes. 'All those men were working at the Lumina site, for a company they call Grannus. Crammed into unsafe accommodation. Come on.'

'No, you come on. It's just their word for it at the moment. But OK, you can bring Forrest in and I'll sign a search warrant for his premises. Don't ask me to be happy about it though. Shit, shit, shit.'

They continued looking at Orentas in his anguish, aware of their voyeurism.

'Poor guy. What will happen to them all now?' Darren asked.

They'll be questioned by the UK Border Force, and after that who knows? They'll have their cases heard; some of them will end up in detention centres or sent back. Some of them have EU passports, for goodness' sake, they were allowed to be here.'

Canter placed a finger and thumb to the bridge of her nose and held it there, eyes closed.

Eager to break the tension, Darren said, 'Apparently the weather's going to break this weekend.'

'Thank God. It's been too long. I've woken up with a headache every day this week, and it just stays all day. It's the air pressure, you can feel it.'

'We'll all be complaining about the rain again next week, won't we? What are we like?'

There was an undeniable new intensity to the atmosphere, something in the air that had become unbearably oppressive. Something had to give, and it would. Thunderstorms were already ripping across Europe, releasing the pressure, with record numbers of lightning strikes, and the weather was about to break here too.

***

Dogs were barking throughout the city. They had been barking all day. If anyone had stopped to listen, they would have noticed that in contrast, no birds were singing, and there was no sign of sparrows, pigeons, seagulls, crows; all had disappeared, taken shelter. The only birds left in the city were the Liver Birds, symbols of the old city that stood firm on their perches on top of the Liver Building. The symbol of a bird had been associated with the city since the thirteenth century, when King Henry III granted the townspeople of Liverpool the right to form a guild with the privileges this came with, including the right to use a common seal. This first depicted a generic bird with a plant sprig in its beak, likely to have been an eagle or possibly a dove. By the seventeenth century the bird's real identity had been forgotten. Nobody knew for sure where 'liver' came from, but it may have been from the Dutch 'lever', or spoonbill. In any case, the statues most resemble the cormorants that were once common seabirds in the river Mersey.

And then when the Liver Building was built in 1911, the liver birds were entrenched as the emblems of Liverpool. The idea was rekindled that the liver was a mythical bird that had once haunted the shoreline. The two statues are proud and majestic, and according to local legend they are a male and female pair; the female looking out to sea, watching for the seamen to return safely home, and the male looking into the city, watching over the seamen's families. Another local legend holds that the birds face away from each other, because if they were to mate and fly away, the city would collapse. They must stay, proud and impassive, to watch over the city. This evening there was no signal from them, only the racing sky behind that sharpened their silhouettes and heightened their motionlessness, giving them a sense of helplessness as heaven and hell, and worse, prepared to loose upon their city.

Two miles to the north on the beach, the Iron Men watched impassively, arms by their sides, as black clouds tumbled in over a sky washed in red and pink. The sea had been as calm as a lake for weeks, the tide often a mile out. When it crept in it would gently bathe the Iron Men in grey, and they would submit to their peaceful twice-daily submerging. But today there had been a crescendo of swell building up since mid-afternoon, and now the high tide whipped up and crashed over the barriers, leaving behind a thick pale yellow foam as it sucked back at speed. The Iron Men stood fast as martyrs lashed to their drowning poles.

The black clouds seemed to billow angrily, as if they were smoke. A faint wind began to blow; almost imperceptible but ominously there. The first breeze in weeks. A slight portentous chill infected the close air, causing people to shudder involuntarily. As thunder rolled and then clapped, families, dog-walkers, revellers, began to half-jog for shelter, and there were queues of traffic to exit the beach car parks. There was no rain yet but people hunched over as they ran, as if to protect themselves from invisible missiles from heaven.

When the sun was completely obscured from view the black clouds, scarlet sky and grey sea formed a three-striped flag as the world's backdrop. The first lightning flashed on the horizon, striking the Irish Sea in some spot that would be forever unknown. A spindled electric finger from heaven, pointing down in judgement at the earth, joining heaven to Earth, plucking a spot for annihilation. Then another, and another, until the whole sky was lit up with flashes and electric branches and the sea was charged. Hundreds of social media videos would be downloaded of the spectacular light show. The sky lit up periodically, unexpectedly, in white flashes that illuminated the turbines of Burbo Bank windfarm out in Liverpool Bay like an old black-and-white movie.

***

Deaconess Margaret Mills was stalking the pews, quoting from the New Testament's most extravagant and apocalyptic text, her beloved Revelation.

"'Woe to you, O Earth and Sea, for the devil has come down to you in great wrath, because he knows his time is short; Let him who hath understanding reckon the number of the beast!" The Revelation, yes. We all know it.'

The quality of the stone that built Argarmeols Hall was such that it had darkened with time, with pollution, and was now almost black in places. The atmosphere was no less dark inside the adjoining St Michael's Church, as Deaconess Margaret conducted her sermon. Perhaps the only upside of the murder scandal that had rocked the Sisters of Grace was an unexpected increase in Deaconess Margaret's evening congregations. They were drawn by morbid curiosity to this sinister convent, where at least one nun was a murderer in the name of religion, and who knew, people wondered, how many of the others were involved. The church had the added bonus of providing a welcome refuge from the heat; its stone walls seemed to emit a cold all of their own. The Deaconess had initially been bemused by this renewed interest; she had expected the church to empty. But she decided to capitalise on it in the way she knew best, and ramped up the theatricality of her sermons even further.

'And what is this number of the Beast?' she roared suddenly into the face of an unsuspecting listener, who cowered back against the next person. Someone muttered 'Six hundred and sixty-six', and she glared at them and stormed over to their pew. 'Is it? Is it? Do you believe everything you read in the Bible?

'Is it one? One poor soul burned to death right here in Crosby village. Is it four? Four forest fires this week, here in Formby! We can smell the ash even here inside the church. Is it eight? Eight men incinerated in the back of a lorry, just a couple of miles from here?

'All these are signifiers. The Devil is here, and he is revealing himself through fire! Do you think this heatwave is a coincidence? Do you?'

Her crazed eyes shot from one face to another, each one looking down in fear that she would make them respond. 'Climate change? Climate change is theurgy. Theurgy. *The interference of deities in human affairs*. She spelled out the definition slowly. Satan is here, and he is revealing himself to us, time and time again, through these miseries. Through bringing the fires of Hell to us on Earth, to remind us of the fate of the Reprobate. The Revelation tells us that Saint John saw a 'sea of glass, mingled with fire'; well that is our city, right now! And as for the cowardly, the faithless, the detestable, as for murderers, the sexually immoral, sorcerers, idolaters, and all liars, their potion will be in the lake that burns with fire and sulphur, which is the second death!'

'And what about the birds?' she shrieked. 'You've all seen them, haven't you! Thousands of birds everywhere at the moment, descending on the city, pigeons stuck in our chimneys, sparrows on our rooves, seagulls in our gardens! There are hundreds of ravens on top of this church, right now! The Revelation tells us that Babylon is "a haunt for every unclean and detestable bird." Well, here we are, in Babylon. Whores that writhe in dens of iniquity, drunken man-beasts. Sound familiar? Babylon, or Liverpool on a Saturday night?'

She returned to her lectern, and stared at the mesmerised congregation for a long time. This preterism, this interpretation of real-world events as Biblical prophecies, had become her favourite tool, and whether or not she believed it herself was largely irrelevant, because it had the desired effect on her listeners.

When the Deaconess spoke again, her voice was quiet and kind.

'But there is hope. Yes, there is hope. For God is here too. And our Lord God also reveals himself through fire. Remember the burning bush? Moses was tending his flock in the wilderness, when the angel of the Lord appeared to him in flames of fire from within the bush. And the Lord God told Moses that he had seen his people's miseries, and that he was with them and would guide them.'

She looked up to the one stained glass window at the back of the church as she recited passages by heart. "And give relief to those who are troubled, and to us as well. This will happen when the Lord Jesus is revealed from heaven in blazing fire with his powerful angels." Thessalonians. Yes,

171

fire is a symbol of the Holy Spirit, so that we may also burn with this fire in our bellies.' She patted her abdomen and sank into a stage whisper. 'Feel it. Feel the holy fire inside of you.'

She paused again, wandering up and down the aisle as her congregation squirmed in confusion at these mixed messages, trying to avoid her gaze. When she reached the front she suddenly swung around, her robes splaying out around her, her eyes wide with rage.

'But do not think for one moment that this Holy Fire is all sweetness and light! Deuteronomy: "For the Lord your God is a consuming fire, a jealous God."

'Thessalonians again: "In flaming fire, inflicting vengeance on those who do not know God and on those who do not obey the gospel of our Lord Jesus."

'Corinthians: "Their work will be shown for what it is, for the Day will bring it to light. It will be revealed with fire, and the fire will test the quality of each person's work."

'The fire will test the quality of each person's work', she repeated. 'This is our test. God is testing us, right now.'

On Evil To Destroy Evil

There is Hell; and then there is that which lies beyond Hell. And therefore speak not of angels that will vanquish demons; speak not of God as a Holy Warrior who shall slay Satan.

For in this universe there are some that are greater in evil than others. Evil's capacity is infinite. And there is One that shall become more powerful than Satan. He shall come in stealth, and he shall come when the time is right.

There shall be a time of Great Tribulation, when the Earth shall be beset by senseless war, famine and terror; when human kills human, when peoples are driven from their homes in droves; when strange beasts and machines ravage the earth and skies. This shall be the work of Satan, attempting to build his new dominion on Earth. And this time shall last for a hundred years and end with the heating up of the earth. And this heating up shall be the sign. That He who is more powerful than Satan is ready to return.

Foolish is he that prays to God in these times of terror, for what use is a God of so-called gentleness and forgiveness? This God does not see the suffering of individuals; he wants not their freedom, only their servitude. Nay, what is prescribed is a great terror; fury, revenge, punishment.

1 Ars Adramelechum 2:13

173

Twelve

In another windowless room beneath a Waterloo sunbed salon, an orange body was thrusting gracelessly, unhurriedly. He was slimy and glistening with pungent tanning oil that reeked of alcohol and chemicals. He liked others to watch, he liked to see the expressions on their faces and to imagine that it was fear, obedience, not boredom or disgust. Slumped on the sofa opposite him and his current reluctant partner were three scantily-clad women, whose faces betrayed that they had all but given up on life. There was no challenge for Max Killy here. He still needed to dominate, to instil fear, and the women he controlled bore the brunt of his business' demise. Here were the last vestiges of his empire, and he would exploit them to the full.

He was beginning to get used to his reduced situation in life; indeed, perhaps in some ways it was a relief. Fewer decisions, fewer dangers, fewer threats. And still enough cash. If he could just get Darren Swift off his back he could relax. It was so frustrating that his name would always be tarnished, when the irony was that he was the one who had gone straight.

He was interrupted by his phone ringing. 'Ee-ar, chuck us that phone, babe.'

'Hello?' He stopped thrusting for a moment, one hand resting on her hip, without withdrawing.

'Hello?' He heard a whispering; so faint as to hardly be there, and his years of nightclub attendance had taken their toll on his hearing. 'Hello?'

One whispered voice became two, became three, became a multitude, as if the world outside the room was filled with whispering voices, insistent, calm yet urgent at the same time. Speaking in tongues, speaking a language unknown yet so familiar as to be something primeval, a language coming from the future and from the past, from the Infinite Space between humanity and the universe.

He was paralysed by a primal terror, by a profound certainty that the world was not as he had imagined it, that he had been blind until now. The whispers were taking him to a place beyond knowledge, and he felt that he was on the very edge and that he must not, must not see what was beyond. And yet he must. That one moment of fear and knowledge became all moments, became the whole of time from the beginning to the end of the world, and then he was blinded by white light and the pain began. A searing pain ripped through his chest and the girl fell from the sofa onto the coffee table with a crash as he withdrew from her roughly.

'Argh, I'm having a heart attack, for fuck's sake call an ambulance…'

The women paused for a moment, considering the various scenarios and possibilities that could play out from this situation. And then it was too late to call an ambulance, because Max threw back his head to roar in pain, but instead of sound there came from his mouth a blast of blue flame, like a blow torch. Immediately after, flames seemed to emerge from his skin, all over, until he was engulfed. He lunged at the nearest girl for help but she and the others ran in terror, so that he fell onto the cheap, flammable sofa. But it did not burn, only his body, and within minutes the only traces of him that remained were his two crucifix necklaces, nestled in a pile of white ash.

***

The sky was a fiery red as Darren, Colette and a search team set off for the Lumina construction office. It was less than five minutes' walk from Canning Place, yet propriety dictated that they went in squad cars, and consequently the journey had taken an irritating forty-five minutes.

'What the fuck is going on?' asked Darren from his

driver's seat. The road was completely cordoned off, and queues of people were swarming towards the Albert Dock area which had become a swathe of white marquees.

'It's the Zeus summer rave. It's the solstice tonight, isn't it, this is their biggest club night of the year, they've taken over the whole dock. Don't tell me you didn't know.'

'Not a clue. I'm totally out of the loop nowadays when it comes to going out.' Darren allowed his focus to drift momentarily to the thought that, one year ago, he and Matt had gone to this party together. He still hadn't managed to speak to him since their argument after the football match, but he was sure everything would be alright.

'Dave's going isn't he?' said Colette. 'With Lacey.'

'Oh, that's why he wanted the evening off! Dave and Lacey.' Darren shook his head affectionately.

'Ah, I think he's fallen for her. It's dead sweet.'

'Yeah, good on him. Anyway, let's get the cars through this road block, this is ridiculous.'

When they arrived at the Lumina 2 site, Shawn Forrest was still there, packing up his briefcase for the end of the day. He stopped and stood up straight, staring at Darren with an indecipherable expression.

'Shawn Forrest, I'm arresting you on suspicion of the manslaughter of the Dock Road Eight, operating poorly maintained commercial vehicles, illegal employment practices, obstruction of justice. And last but by no means least, human trafficking.'

Forrest looked implacable as he said, 'Think very carefully about what you're doing, Detective Inspector Swift.'

'You're not in a position to threaten me, Mr. Forrest. We also have a warrant to search these premises,' he gestured to the officers behind him, 'so if you'd like to come with me, they can get started.'

They took him out to the squad cars, Forrest's face betraying a thunderous expression as he tried to conceal himself from the gawpers that crowded the streets. Darren drove with Colette in the passenger seat and Forrest in the back. When he looked in the rear view mirror Forrest was staring at him menacingly.

Back at Canning Place, Shawn Forrest waited in a cell while Darren joined Superintendent Canter and several of her superiors to discuss the minefield that was how to question him.

Canter said, 'So we've possibly got him on human trafficking, manslaughter......'

'And murder.'

'Darren.'

'I think he killed those eight men on purpose.'

'For what possible reason? Surely that would—'

'I think he was trying to frame Max Killy. The one enemy he hadn't managed to destroy. Hiring Max's nephew Stuart, putting up his workers two steps from Killy's gym, the things he implied in his speech, the threats, the...'

There were other reasons – reasons too... what? Supernatural? Demonic? – for Darren to explain. Those people had been expendables, and Darren's fear, exacerbated by the strange expression on Forrest's face, was that this was not over.

There was a knock on the door; the search team had returned from the Lumina office with a seemingly crucial piece of evidence.

'You'll probably need to see this before you even start, Ma'am.'

They held up a clear plastic evidence bag that was filled with dog-eared passports.

'Taken from the safe in his office.'

'Shit.'

'So Shawn Forrest is an illegal gangmaster.'

'Worse than that. He's a human trafficker. So it's true.'

There was another knock, an officer informing them that Forrest wanted to make a request.

'I'll go,' said Darren, getting up.

'I'd like to make a phone call please, Detective. I believe that's my right.'

'Actually it's at our discretion. But I believe your lawyer is on the way, Mr Forrest.'

'I'm not calling my lawyer.'

Fair enough, thought Darren. The call would be recorded anyway, so with any luck it would be incriminating. Darren escorted him to the station's reception area, where all the staff watched in silence as Forrest leaned against the desk and calmly dialled a number, never taking his eyes off Darren. What was that expression? Was it amusement? Triumph? It was disconcerting in a way Darren could not define, and it made him extremely uneasy which, he supposed, was the intention. The call was answered and Forrest simply said, staring at Darren as he did so,

'It's time. Do it now.'

A clear plastic wallet filled with passports landed with a slap. Darren threw it down on the interview room table as he sat down across from Forrest. He was able to summon all his confidence because surely Forrest was finished now.

'Ten passports found in your office safe. Ten passports matching the identity of ten men living at 8 Beacon Street, all of whom say they were working at Lumina 2.'

Forrest was silent, bizarrely smug. *How long can he keep this up?* thought Darren.

'Why were you keeping their passports in a safe?'

Finally Forrest spoke. 'Exactly that, to keep them safe. Their accommodation isn't secure, strangers sharing a house, not a nice area of Liverpool; it was for their sake, for safe-keeping.'

'Yeah, right. So they were all working illegally on the Lumina 2 site.'

'No, that's totally wrong. They all had proper contracts and papers, employed by Forrest Construction. Our lawyers will be providing them.'

'I'm sure they will. But these men claim they were employed by a company called Grannus. The same company that owned that burnt out truck. What do you know about Grannus?'

'I've never heard of it. I've told you that before.'

'Of course you did.'

'Look, Detective, this is all ridiculous, it's going to be cleared up in no time and you're going to look very stupid.'

This was going to be a long haul, thought Darren, as he took a moment to look through his notes. Surely Forrest didn't have a leg to stand on, but he was remarkably confident, even for him, considering the severity of the situation.

'Ok, Darren,' said Forrest, smiling. 'Let's level. I'll tell you what I know about Grannus. Grannus is the Celtic god of healing. I believe you know a lot about Swiss gods. Of various types.'

Darren looked up suddenly. 'What did you say?'

At that moment Canter knocked and entered, maintaining formality in front of the suspect. 'Sorry to interrupt, Detective Inspector Swift. Can I have a word?'

Darren stepped out, dreading yet half-expecting her to say that Forrest was free, off the hook, or that he himself was being removed from the case. But as soon as he was in the corridor he became aware of the sound of sirens, many sirens blaring, competing wails in the air outside.

'What's going on out there?'

'Darren there's a huge fire at the Lumina 2 site. Apparently it started with an explosion and now it's a fireball. Never seen anything like it, the whole sky is lit up. I don't know what it means but I'm already thinking insurance fraud. Did you listen to Forrest's phone call? Did he get someone to torch the place? Anyway, better press the pause button on this interview for now.'

They looked through the mirrored glass window into the interview room, where Forrest sat very still, with that indefinable expression on his face.

'Darren,' said Canter, without taking her eyes off Forrest. 'Is Matt on duty tonight?'

Prayers To Burn Thine Enemy

I.

O Samarian Devil, Commander of Hell
Chancellor of the Infernal Regions
See how we burn children at your altars.

II.

O King of Fire, Keeper of the Furnaces,
Idol god of Sepharvaim
You are the true Majestic One.

III.

Foe or God, thou shalt become greater than Satan
We bring forth this fire to cast out our enemies
We bring forth this fire to raise our King above Satan.

IV.

With this flame I bring forth the Eternal Fire
With this flame I open the Furnaces of Hell
Holy water cannot quench this fire.

V.

Bring Forth The Eternal Fire
Bring Forth The Eternal Fire
Bring Forth The Eternal Fire
Bring Forth The Eternal Fire
Bring Forth The Eternal Fire
Bring Forth The Eternal Fire
Bring Forth The Eternal Fire
Bring Forth The Eternal Fire.

1 Ars Adramelechum 2:13

Thirteen

The summer solstice, marker of the seasons, when the sun is at its highest point in the celestial sphere. That existential moment marked by few in our times, was almost over, and tonight rather than being the lightest evening of the year, it was the darkest it had been in weeks. The elusive and longed-for clouds had finally descended to obscure the height of the sun. Past the docks, a crowd of one thousand people were mostly oblivious to the thunder and lightning, entertained by another sound and light show; the thudding beats and strobe lights of Zeus' open-air summer rave.

At an altar of sorts, built of monitors and speakers, above the crowd, a DJ presided whipping one hand in the air as the other operated controls on a huge mixer board. Two thousand hands were raised in the air and the crowd jumped as one, creating its own pneumatic uplift force. The bass pummelled like a collective heartbeat.

Dave and Lacey bounced in the middle of the crowd; they embraced and then looked up to the sky screwing up their eyes and laughing as the first heavy drops of rain began to fall. Cheers erupted around them as the rain fell heavier and heavier, and soon hair was plastered to faces that streamed with water and joy as people shrieked with laughter. The sound of thunder was drowned by the amplifiers, the lightning by the artificial strobes. Fireworks had been planned for months, and the organisers had decided to go ahead regardless of the rain. A single rocket launched straight into the air heralded the beginning of a series of multi-coloured explosions in the sky; comets, brocade crowns, giant Catherine wheels. It was magnificent. Perhaps too magnificent, thought Dave, never a fan of fireworks, as he wondered if they weren't being launched a little too close to nearby building site.

And then suddenly the fireworks stopped, the cheers stopped, the bouncing stopped, and the music carried on at first and then tapered off itself. Because a huge bang shook the arena, a bang much louder than thunder, too real to be a firework. And it was immediately followed by a blaze that lit up the sky behind the arena, the flames reflecting in every face that turned towards the city. The shrieks of joy stopped in a moment of collective shock, then turned to shrieks of horror.

'That's the Lumina 2!'

Dave instinctively put his arms around Lacey to protect her, as panic set in amongst the revellers.

'Oh my god, Dave.'

'It's alright, it's just a building site, there won't have been anyone in there. But we need to get out of here before the whole structure collapses. Come on.'

They pushed their way through the crowds that swarmed towards the emergency exits, Dave glancing back all the while at the gathering inferno behind them. When they finally reached a place of safety, they joined the hundreds of other faces that gazed up mesmerised by the flames. The tower of fire was strangely rainbow-coloured, and it was hard to believe but there seemed to be flames of blue, purple and green mingled with the torrent of red and gold. People blinked and blamed their bizarre vision on the acrid smoke that stung their eyes. Some were screaming, coughing and covering their faces in agony, since the fumes were not ordinary smoke but seemed poisonous. *A sea of glass, mingled with fire.*

'It shouldn't have gone up like that,' said Dave in disbelief at the billowing flames and multitudes of mini explosions. 'It was just an empty shell, scaffolding. How could it be like that?'

He couldn't tell Lacey, but he knew that Darren had gone to arrest Shawn Forrest that evening. This couldn't possibly be a coincidence. Perhaps he had got someone to torch the place, perhaps it was an insurance scam, or something to do with destroying evidence.

***

Her lecture over, Helen made her way to her new church, the Angel of Liverpool, a short walk from the university. For the first time in weeks it wasn't too hot to walk, and she enjoyed the cooler temperature, hoping she would make it to the church before the rain started. It had been so long, it was as if she could hardly remember what rain felt like. When she arrived, the chatter amongst her fellow singers was all about the weather.

Choir practice was now her favourite hour of the week. Her voice had been stifled for so long, by the convent, by her self-imposed martyrdom, and the novelty of singing was far from wearing off. What on earth had she been thinking, forbidding herself from making music all those years? After all, as St Augustine said in one of his many beautiful sermons, 'To sing is to pray twice.' She had so many plans for the choir, so many musical ideas; and she often toyed with the idea of calling Mikko to share them with him. When she had suggested to the choir master that they tackle Monteverdi's *Vespro della Beata Vergine*, he had raised his eyebrows and chuckled 'Well, you're nothing if not ambitious, Helen. I think *Shine, Jesus, Shine* is more our thing here.' But Helen had arrived at a moment in her life when she felt that anything and everything was possible. She had wasted too much time to shy away from a challenge, and too many years of not listening to music to avoid that which was the most beautiful. She explained to the choir master that the beauty of Monteverdi's seventeenth century masterpieces was that they could be adapted to whatever instruments and voices were at hand. So now he waved his baton with astonished glee as the local amateur choir sung their way through heavenly plainsong melodies that rolled into each other in a glorious tapestry of sound.

The choir raised their voices to the glory of God, and Helen flung hers out the strongest so that it rang out at the top of the exquisite harmonies. Untrained since the age of fourteen, her voice retained an unusual purity of tone, and she allowed herself a small amount of pride at being the new 'star' of the choir. She recognised that her choice of the *Vespro della Beata Vergine* wasn't simply due to the beauty of its musical composition; it was the subject matter too. It was one of the many musical settings of the *Magnificat*, recorded in St. Luke's Gospel, when Mary visited her cousin Elizabeth, who was pregnant with John the Baptist. At Mary's greeting, Elizabeth felt the baby move within her, and was filled with the Holy Spirit. Mary's response was the *Magnificat*, and Helen was moved by the thought of Mary with the incredible secret she held in her own belly.

My soul doth magnify the Lord
And my spirit hath rejoiced in God my Saviour
For he hath regarded the lowliness of his handmaiden,
For behold, from henceforth all generations shall call me blessed.
For he that is might hath magnified me; and holy is his name.

The *Magnificat* had rarely featured in Sisters of Grace services, which was just as well perhaps for the nuns who had denied themselves the chance to ever feel what Elizabeth and Mary had felt. But Helen had been thinking about it a lot recently. Or rather, she had been thinking about babies. The child of Andrew Shepherd and his experimental subject Chelsea McAllister, the child supposedly born without sin, was alive and in Liverpool. Whether Helen believed that meant anything at all was perhaps the ultimate test of her faith. The only person with whom she could possibly discuss it rationally was Darren, and she was afraid in case he dismissed it, because there was something undeniably magical about the dream of it.

Helen also thought about herself. For the first time in her adult life she could finally imagine the possibility of one day, perhaps, bearing a child herself. She was thirty-three, and supposed she was sensing that biological clock which women always talked about. But the processes to be gone through seemed insurmountable. How would she even begin? With a boyfriend, she supposed, and if only she could stop thinking about Mikko she might be able to consider how to go about that.

As the rain came down, sporadically at first then insistently, it hammered on the church's iron roof and built into a crescendo of clattering white noise. The choir instinctively sang louder to prevent themselves being drowned out. Above the church door, in Helen's direct line of sight, a round, intricately cut stained glass window was duller than usual due to the dark grey clouds that had descended behind it. And then colours began to flicker in the glass; the tones reddened, as if there were flames behind. It wasn't possible, and yet it looked so much like fire. Helen was suddenly seized by a shudder of mortal fear; the last time she had felt like this was when she learnt of Andrew Shepherd's discovery of the OS1 gene; when she had learnt of the possibility that fate not only existed, but that it could be changed. Something was not quite right, and for some reason it had to do with Darren.

***

There was no point in trying to drive, all the roads were blocked. Darren ran across Strand Street, across the Albert Dock car park, weaving through groups of people escaping the Zeus party, hurdling over bollards and railings. The rain was torrential and the gutters were already filled with puddles and water streamed down the tarmac and down his face so that he had to continually rub his eyes in order to see. Black clouds blotted a deep crimson sky.

As he got closer he had to push past straggles of people, which became crowds of people, who were scurrying about from the abandoned outdoor rave. As he neared the Lumina site it became hard to breath, and the smoke had a strange acrid quality to it and made the rain drops taste foul in his mouth. A cordon had already been set up and Darren moved along it frantically, back and forth. This was a fire like no other he had ever seen. Mushrooms of flame puffed out of windows continually like a species of mad science experiment. Suddenly a boom was accompanied by a particularly large billow of flame which threw the body of a fireman out from a window low to the ground, causing screams to erupt from onlookers.

Darren ducked under the cordon and ran towards the blaze but was stopped in his tracks by a firefighter. The man was wearing a mask which he took off, wincing in the acid air, to speak to Darren.

'Stop there, mate, what are you doing?'

Darren was looking over his shoulders frantically, when he realised he knew this man – it was a colleague of Matt.

'Where's Matt?'

The firefighter, who had hold of Darren's arms, paused for too long. 'He's in there. His was the first team to arrive. It wasn't going off like this then, it was manageable. It doesn't make any sense, the way it's burning up like this, we can't get it under control. We've lost contact with most of them.'

Darren looked up to where mini-explosions continued the job of destroying all trace of Lumina 2. It was now just a skeletal black frame, tottering and crumbling, and soon, like the body of Eliza Bektashi weeks before, it would disappear into nothing, destroying all that was inside.

***

The sun went down, a red orb diving beneath the clouds over the River Mersey. The baby finally tired as Justine Kuper danced his little body around the room, cradling his head with one hand, her lips pressed against the downy hair on his skull. He looked at the mobiles that swayed above his crib, the long shadows of evening that cast against his designer wallpaper and furniture, and his eyes grew heavy-lidded and finally closed. His skull rested heavily on Justine's shoulder blade, and with a final touch of her lips to his head she lowered him gently into his bed. His arms and legs splayed out like the chalk outline at a crime scene. Justine smiled and watched him for a few moments, checking that he had settled. She could feel that the storm was coming; any minute the rain would begin to fall.

Sure that he was deeply asleep now, Justine moved over to the window to close the curtains. Across the road she could see another family busy with their bedtime routine; the Ghosh household, always filled with foster children and now with a new baby, only a few weeks older than her own. The evening was dark enough now that she could see the silhouettes of Mr and Mrs Ghosh at their upstairs window. Their curtains were open and they were showing the baby their elder children who were running in the front garden, shrieking and splashing through a paddling pool in a final outburst of energy before bed. It was far away across the road, but the baby in the window suddenly seemed to look directly at her. Justine shuddered and fingered the diamond pendant around her neck, twisting it vertically so that the symbol was transformed from an infinity into a number eight. The baby's gaze turned from Justine down to the Kupers' driveway, where the peacock was standing in full plumage, quivering its feathers. Justine's mobile phone vibrated in her pocket. 'Hello? Ok, nice one.'

She put the phone back in her pocket, closed the curtains emphatically, and moved over to the chest of drawers on the other side of the room. The bottom drawer was locked but she reached underneath to where a key had been sellotaped to the underside of the chest. Justine knew her mother would never stumble upon it there. She opened the drawer and methodically took out its contents as a priest laying out the equipment for a service. She lay them on top of the chest of drawers, placing them slowly and reverentially with each item equidistant from the one next to it and from the edge of the wooden surface. A small bronze bowl, polished on the outside but burnished black on the inside from previous use. A white candle on a polished bronze stand, decorated with dried rivulets of wax. A single match taken from a packet; a little wooden cross that she selected from a box full of them; a mobile phone taken from a small pile of handsets. A photo of a building, a large prefabricated structure encased in green. And a huge book, its uneven pages yellowed and worn, its binding a light brown, leathery material. Justine had to use both hands to lift the book out of the drawer, and when she placed it down she paused for a moment and closed her eyes, stroking the cold, clammy front cover of the book with one hand, fingering her number eight pendant with the other.

Then she placed the photo in the bowl, and held up the cross to the candle until it caught alight. She watched it burn down to her fingers and then dropped it into the bowl, to burn along with the photo. She picked up the phone, switched it on and as soon as it sprang to life she dialled the number for the night watch desk at Lumina 2. When the security guard answered she began to whisper, firmly, urgently.

O Lord Adramelech, who shalt become greater than Satan
I desire the vengeance of the Eternal Fire
With this flame I open the Furnaces of Hell
Holy water cannot quench this fire

Bring Forth The Eternal Fire
Bring Forth The Eternal Fire
Bring Forth The Eternal Fire
Bring Forth The Eternal Fire
Bring Forth The Eternal Fire
Bring Forth The Eternal Fire
Bring Forth The Eternal Fire
Bring Forth The Eternal Fire

As she whispered, she felt that other voices were joining her on the line, breaking through the static, the fuzz, myriad voices from across time and space. She gazed at the tiny fire that flickered in the bowl, and just for the briefest moment, her eyes changed. Those vacant eyes that never properly met your own. The black of her pupils shrank to nothing, and her green irises turned to flame. What had appeared shallow now became labyrinthine, a kaleidoscope of fire that plunged into the depths beyond hell in the infinite space. And then it was gone.

Epilogue

July; and the sky was a seemingly constant white-grey. The grass was returning to green, the beaches and parks emptying out, schools open again for the last few weeks of term. The heatwave was a mere scar on the collective memory now, the sleepless nights, sweltering workplaces and solastalgia forgotten in favour of more pleasant memories; the glowing skin, bare feet, picnics and beer gardens. And there had been no collective sigh of relief in Liverpool when the weather finally broke, because it had been marred by the Lumina 2 fire.

Above Sandhills Cemetery, the sky hung appropriately low and grey, signifying that there would be no let-up in the relentless rain today. Umbrellas formed a sea of black around the memorial, and spattering rain drops on their tops muffled the sounds of the celebrant, of the crying from Matt's mother.

Darren had made himself numb; it was the only way to get through the day. The fire service had arranged everything, and it had been overwhelming; the fire engines that lined the street, the coffin mounted on a turntable ladder vehicle for the journey from the fire station, the crowds that waited in the rain, the blanket of umbrellas. This was the first of three firefighter funerals that would take place this week, and all three had been awarded posthumous medals of bravery.

As bagpipes played, Darren and five of Matt's colleagues, chosen as the honour guard, had carried the coffin, draped in the fire service flag, to the graveside, and the service was carried out. Matt had been too young to leave a will, but they knew he would have wanted something simple, and definitely wouldn't have wanted to be in a churchyard. The memorial was a simple block of slate, roughly cut, and in front of the stone had been placed Matt's gleaming helmet. The back of the stone was cloaked in the flag. Everything was sodden. Darren wondered whether this bleak plain of death was appropriate, or just too desperately lonely to contemplate. In any case now they had reached the final goodbye, before the nightmare of the wake where he would finally have to face people.

'As we say our final goodbye to Matthew,' said the celebrant, 'son, brother, fiancé, friend, hero – we celebrate his life and the joy that he brought to the lives of others, and we remember that he died doing the job that he loved, in the service of his community. There will now be a moment of silence.'

Eventually the outer mourners, many of them in fire service uniform, began to peel away. Colette and Canter took their leave, with backwards glances towards Darren who remained stationary in front of the memorial as people queued to pay their respects.

Colette and Canter slow-walked down the concrete path towards the cemetery gates, Colette more gingerly as she wasn't used to daytime heels, both wondering if they should have gone and said something to Darren. But what else was there to say? They would see him at the wake.

'Beautiful service.'

'Yeah. Beautiful.'

Colette took a couple of deep breaths before saying,

'Ma'am, is it true that Forrest is going to get off? I heard he's been released without charge. How can that be possible?'

Canter stopped to face her, looking surreptitiously from side to side and signalling for them both to lower their voices as people were walking past. Then she sighed sympathetically.

'Yes. Yes, it looks as if he will get off. There's nothing on him. The sheeting that covered the Lumina 2 was mis-sold to Forrest Group, it was inflammable and it went up with a spark from the solstice fireworks at the Zeus rave. So if anyone is going to be prosecuted, it's the sheeting manufacturer. And the city council for poor health and safety at the fireworks display.'

'That's the official reason, yeah. But my arse. It was insurance fraud. You know it.'

'Colette. We've got no evidence. And he's got the best lawyers…'

'What about those workers in that house! I found them, Ma'am! And he had their passports locked away.'

'He said it was just for safekeeping. They all turned out to have proper contracts. Plus, his lawyer is arguing that it was illegal entry and therefore inadmissible evidence, since you forced the door.'

'But you can't possibly believe that, Ma'am.'

'Look, I don't like it. There's something not right about it. But right now—'

'Don't tell me. Your hands are tied.'

Canter opened her mouth, and then stopped herself. This wasn't the place to reprimand anyone. She sighed.

'Colette, do you think Darren will be alright? I haven't managed to speak to him properly. He's on three weeks' compassionate leave.'

'I went over to his place the other day. Helped him go through all the cards and messages, you know. Threw away most of the food people had sent over. It was awful. He's at the angry stage right now. I mean, manic angry. He had all this research. Crazy stuff he got from the internet. Says he's not going back to the police.'

'He'll come round. He's going to be a great detective.'

'Ma'am, if the police don't go after Forrest, Darren will, I'm telling you.'

Darren was soaked, a raincoat over his suit, his trainers squelching in the grass. The rain that streamed down his face took the place of tears that he forced himself to hold back.

'Darren. I'm so very sorry.' Helen appeared alongside Darren and reached up to place an arm around his shoulder. They fell into a hug and it was the very first time their bodies had touched, and Darren thought he might break at this moment. But he steeled himself and looked at her. They shared a forbidden knowledge. A suspicion that there were depths to this that were perhaps beyond human comprehension. They hugged awkwardly under Helen's umbrella.

'Helen. This isn't over.'

'No. It isn't.'

There was nothing else to say, so she squeezed his shoulders and took her leave.

Darren stood for as long as he could. Took a deep breath and braced himself for the grim reality of the wake which had to be endured. He took a final look at the memorial. As he was about to turn away, there was a silent black flapping, and a small flock of ravens landed on the grass next to him. Eight ravens. They stood in one line, occasionally blinking in the rain, nodding, shaking the water from their feathers. Looking at Darren. And then in one single movement they opened their wings and took flight. Darren watched as they shrank to dots and then disappeared into the grey.

He turned around and walked towards the cemetery gates. The fire engines and cars had left, leaving only the last straggling groups of walkers who were almost at the end of the road.

But there was one car left, parked on the other side of the road, opposite the cemetery gate, and it was instantly recognizable. A red Ferrari. There weren't many of those around in Crosby. And there was Thomas Kuper, standing on the pavement with his legs apart, in a broad stance with arms folded. Darren couldn't be sure if it was threatening or awkward. Under Kuper's raincoat he was wearing a black suit and black tic, as if he had been planning to attend the funeral. But Darren hadn't seen him amongst the mourners or the crowds; surely he would have had the decency to stay away?

Darren turned and began walking away towards the wake, shaking his head in a grimace, muttering, 'For fuck's sake.'

But Kuper started and dashed across the road, dodging an oncoming car as he did so. He caught up with Darren, who continued walking, so he got in front of him and held him by the arms. Darren shook his head, refusing to look him in the eye, looking anywhere but at him.

'What are you doing here? This is so not the time. Just leave me alone.'

'Darren, look at me, please.'

Darren finally looked into Kuper's eyes, and he saw that they were scared.

'I'm sorry, I'm sorry. But Darren, please. I need your help.'

Fantastic Books
Great Authors

CROOKED
CAT

Meet our authors and discover
our exciting range:

- Gripping Thrillers
- Cosy Mysteries
- Romantic Chick-Lit
- Fascinating Historicals
- Exciting Fantasy
- Young Adult and Children's
  Adventures

Visit us at:
www.crookedcatbooks.com

Join us on facebook:
www.facebook.com/crookedcatbooks

36203693R00120

Printed in Poland
by Amazon Fulfillment
Poland Sp. z o.o., Wrocław